THE FOGGIEST

They found their way on to the field beyond the cottage. Rachel climbed through a gap in the dry stone wall. She moved very slowly, knowing that the ground was covered in debris, knowing that she couldn't afford to make a sound. She reached the tree at the end of the pond and rested against it for a moment. An arm shot out from behind the tree and a hand covered her mouth.

"Don't make a sound."

Also by David Belbin:

Point

THE FOGGIEST

David Belbin

■ SCHOLASTIC

For Sue

Scholastic Children's Books,
Commonwealth House, 1-19 New Oxford Street,
London WC1A 1NU, UK
a division of Scholastic Ltd
London ~ New York ~ Toronto ~ Sydney ~ Auckland

First published in the UK by Scholastic Publications Ltd, 1990
This edition published by Scholastic Ltd, 1997

ISBN 0 590 19376 7

Typeset by AKM Associates (UK) Ltd, Southall, London
Printed by Cox and Wyman Ltd, Reading, Berks.

10 9 8 7 6 5 4 3 2 1

Chapter One

A classic Christmas Day. It had snowed and it was going to snow again. Roger Deakin stared out of the Weather Station window, wishing he was at home with the kids, making a snowman in the garden. Although doubtless they were in front of the telly, watching *The Wizard of Oz* or whatever was on this afternoon. It had been hard explaining to them that he'd drawn the short straw this Christmas. Harder explaining to his wife, Elsie. But the worst thing was that he had to share the duty with Stan Brown.

Stan had volunteered, of course. He volunteered for all the unsocial shifts. He had no home life, no social life, not even with his workmates. His only love was the weather computer. A perfect employee for a Weather Research Station, but hardly the sort of bloke you wanted to spend Christmas with.

Roger checked his monitors, then settled down to catch up on the week's newspapers. " 'No early election', says Prime Minister." No real news. Roger was just working up to the Christmas crossword when the blow came. It split his head open and sent him reeling across the floor. He didn't wake up for a long time.

Stan Brown tapped on a window. Then he unbolted the one outside door and let in a balaclavaed man wearing a green parka, who shook the snow from his boots. Together, the men dragged Roger Deakin into a side room, where Brown injected him with a strong sedative. Next he took a package from his locker, brightly wrapped to look like a Christmas present. The other man opened it.

While Harvey was setting up the transmitter, Brown made several phonecalls, releasing various station officers from their duties. Sat at home on a Christmas Day, none was in a mood to question the nature of the "breakdown". They were glad to get an extended holiday. Deakin's wife was less pleased when Brown explained that her husband had been called away on highly confidential business. But these things were part of the job, as Brown explained.

There was only one person Brown couldn't get through to – Jack Gunn, the new Chief Scientist. His old phone had been disconnected and no one was answering at his new home, so he couldn't have moved in yet. Still, Gunn wasn't due to start for three days. By then it would be impossible to travel. Brown decided to leave it. There were more important things that needed immediate attention. David Harvey had made contact with Control.

A crackle of static preceded the distant voice.

"Acknowledge."

"Receiving you. Awaiting instructions."

"Is takeover complete?"

"Complete. Without casualties."

"Very well. Begin. Over."

"Over and out."

There was silence on the airwaves. The two men glanced at each other, then went to work.

"How far is it now?"

Dad groaned. Rachel turned to Matthew in the back of the car and snapped:

"That's the third time you've asked in fifteen minutes! We'll be there when we're there!"

"Don't try and sound like Mum."

Rachel shivered, then shut up. Dad stared ahead at the motorway traffic, his face blank, the way it always went when you mentioned Mum. She'd been dead for six months.

It was Boxing Day. Christmas had been awful. Gran had insisted they stay in their tiny flat when all they really wanted was to ignore the festival. Dad had suggested making the move to Derbyshire on Boxing Day, when the roads wouldn't be crowded for once, though Gran had argued that a full Christmas was "important for the children". Rachel didn't feel like a

3

child any more. She'd just turned sixteen. Matt, on the other hand, behaved like a baby, even though he was only three years younger. He'd woken up at five on Christmas Day and unwrapped all his presents. The tags were mixed up so you couldn't tell what was from whom for the thank-you letters. And no one even told him off.

Although a lot of people were still on holiday, the M1 was busy. Dad had to keep changing lanes as massive lorries flashed their lights at the back of them. Rachel would never learn to drive. The van that ran over her mother had seen to that. Mum had hated cars too – said they were dirty and dangerous. She'd tried to persuade Dad to do without one, but he'd needed it for his job. Now they were moving to the middle of nowhere, he'd need it even more.

Radio One was on. They were playing something old, tuneless and noisy. "This is rubbish," said Rachel. "Can I turn it off, Dad?"

Her father, she noticed, was tapping his fingers against the steering wheel. "I love this one," he told her. "It's REM. 'Pop Song '89'. A classic."

Rachel endured the song by trying to decipher the chorus, which was about the government and the weather. Weird. But Dad loved old rock music. At home he listened to all the stuff from the Seventies – Springsteen, Sex Pistols, Steely Dan. Most of it was just noise to Rachel. She stared ahead, trying to imagine her new life in Derbyshire, living in a cottage she hadn't yet seen. The night sky was clear and held a crescent moon, the sort you expected a witch to fly across with a broomstick. Dad would be OK, with his important new job. Matt would get by; he was only in the second year. But Rachel had messed up school so badly that she was having to go down a year. Also, she'd already missed a term at her new school, so she'd have mounds of GCSE coursework to catch up on, despite being a year older than the other kids. It wasn't fair.

"That's all we need!"

Suddenly, a thick fog had descended on the motorway and they could see little further than the car in front of them. Dad braked sharply, reducing their speed from seventy to fifty. The lorry behind screeched its brakes, almost hitting them.

"Turn the radio off, Rachel. I need to concentrate."

Rachel did as she was told. Matt curled up in the back, keeping his fear to himself. The fog was getting thicker. It seemed to swirl in front of them, then settle, as though they were in the middle of a cloud. All Rachel could make out of the car in front were its tail lights.

"Shouldn't you put the headlights on full beam?"

Dad shook his head.

"It wouldn't help. The light reflects off the fog, so we can't see as far. In fact, we'd be able to make out more if we turned our lights off, but then no one could see us."

Rachel wasn't sure this made sense to her, but Dad was a meteorologist, among other things. He ought to know.

"How far is it now?"

This time Dad didn't groan and Rachel made no comment. Their speed was down to thirty miles an hour, and falling.

"It's the exit after next, Matt. I don't know how far. Not long."

But the next exit was a long time coming. Snow turned to sludge kept spraying the windscreen as other vehicles passed them at dangerous speeds. Rachel almost missed the sign when it came.

"Doesn't that say 'Loughborough'?"

"I think you're right. That's our turning. Can't have seen the last one."

Without signalling, Dad swerved off the motorway on to the slip road. Behind them a lorry sounded its horn angrily.

"Well spotted, Rachel."

At the roundabout, they took the A512 going away from Loughborough. It was narrow for an A road and much quieter than the M1. Tall trees concealed the landscape, but when they went you still couldn't see anything. It was just too foggy. Rachel made out a lorry park and the Dunlop factory on the right – little else. They'd gone two or three miles before Dad spoke again:

"I think we turn here."

"Are we nearly there now?"

"Only a mile or two, Matt."

The road they turned on to was narrow and unlit. You couldn't tell where the road ended and the verge began, or where a ditch was covered by old snow. A couple of times, the Fiesta scraped something on the side. They took another turning, and this time the road was even narrower – a one-car track with an occasional widening for vehicles to pass. Dad looked apprehensive. Rachel found herself getting scared.

Suddenly, another car lunged out of the mire at them. Dad braked sharply, but they still nearly clashed. It was a Landrover, half a dozen white and red headlights shining at them, towering over the tiny Fiesta. Cautiously, Dad began to back up, but the Landrover simply drove around them, bounding over the hedge on their right as though it were a few weeds.

"Farmers!" Dad muttered. "No respect for hedgerows."

They drove on, passing nothing. After a mile or so, they reached a crossroads. The lane going one way was wider than the one they were on. The road ahead looked narrower still, just a dirt track.

"I don't remember this," Dad said. "Rachel, get out and have a look if there's a sign, will you?"

Rachel wished she had a coat to hand, yet, when she got out, it felt more damp than cold. There was a signpost to the right of the crossroads, but it had been bent out of its original position, and she could only guess which way it had originally pointed. One of the four arms pointed to "Nether Hulme ½ mile". The cottage was in Nether Hulme. Rachel sighed.

"What's wrong?"

"The sign's been knocked round. I can't tell which way it should go."

7

"I'll have a look."

Dad got out, though Rachel could have saved him the bother. Clearly the sign had been knocked over, uprooted, then put back in. Whichever way they went, it would be guesswork.

Dad examined the sign.

"Maybe if I check against the map book . . ."

Rachel felt someone coming up behind her.

"Matt . . .?"

She turned round. Matt was still in the car. She'd have heard him get out. There was something moving by the dry stone wall that ran along the road to their left. Some kind of animal perhaps. A large black shape loomed over the wall. Rachel tried to adjust to being in the country. Probably a cow. The shape came over the wall towards her, a large, moving lump.

"Dad!"

It stopped. Dad looked over from the car where he'd gone for the map book.

"Hello?"

"You look like you're lost."

The voice was gruff, with an accent that Rachel could only identify as northern. It was not friendly, but not exactly unfriendly either. The shape came closer – a large man, with a thick overcoat and heavy-set face, all but covered by brown straggly hair and a full beard. When he was almost upon Rachel, she saw that his eyes were a penetrating blue. Dad joined her.

"We're trying to get to Nether Hulme. Do you know it?"

"Aye. You've gone past it."

"I thought as much. We must have missed a turning."

"Easily done in this weather."

"Yes. Could you show me . . .?"

"I can, but you're liable to miss it again unless you know what you're looking for."

Dad hesitated. Rachel knew what he was going to say next and she wished he wouldn't. On the other hand, they had to find their new home.

"I don't suppose you could see your way to . . .?"

"I've got nothing better to do."

Rachel opened the door for the man.

"You can have my seat. I'll go in the back."

As he came closer she saw that his coat was ripped and the scarf round his neck filthy. The man was a common tramp. She'd seen many of them in London, homeless people living in cardboard boxes, scavenging off the capital's leftovers. She'd thought that, by moving here, they were getting away from that kind of thing.

Matt opened the back passenger door for her. They exchanged repulsed glances, Matt shrivelling up his pudgy face. The tramp's smell filled the car – a dense, earthy odour. But Dad talked to him as though they were equals. It was embarrassing.

"You from round here?"

"Round and about."

"I'm Jack Gunn. My children Matt and Rachel in the back. We've bought the Low Farm cottage at Nether Hulme."

"Aye. I know."

This sounded menacing to Rachel, but Dad breezed on.

"Yes, I suppose everyone knows everyone's business round here."

"You're going to work at that weather place no one's supposed to have heard about over in Upper Hulme. Turn ten yards on your left."

Dad darted a nervous expression at the tramp, then smiled as he turned the wheel.

"That's right. I'm taking over as Chief Scientist. It's quite exciting. The place isn't exactly secret, though. It doesn't get publicised, that's all."

"Same thing."

"I suppose you're right. You didn't tell us your name."

"Stone. They call me Stone."

"No first name?"

"Not any more. Turn just on your right here."

Ahead of them was the cottage. Even in the fog, Rachel recognised it from the photographs. She squeezed Matt's arm. For the first time in the holiday, he smiled. They all got out.

"You've been a tremendous help. Can I offer you a drink or something?"

The two men talked for a minute as Matt and Rachel went up to the front door of their new home. Then Dad came and unlocked it.

"He's not coming in, is he?" Matt asked.

Dad put a finger to his mouth and shook his head. Inside, Rachel said, "He scared me."

10

Dad switched on the light and she stared at the passage. The building was three hundred years old, and looked it.

"Nothing to be afraid of. We're home."

Rachel pushed the door shut behind them. Outside, the tramp had already disappeared into the thick fog, back to wherever he had come from.

Chapter Two

Rachel was dreaming that she was on the phone to her best friend, Katie. They were talking about some party they were both going to, like they did last Christmas. Then Katie said:

"But how are you going to get there, Rachel? You live in Derbyshire."

And Rachel woke. It was just after seven. She and Matt had gone to bed early the night before, tired after the journey. She'd hardly noticed her new room. It was big and bare. And cold. The cottage had no central heating. She thought about turning the electric fire on, but decided it would be quicker to get up and dress. She wanted some company.

Stepping into her jeans, Rachel pulled her thickest Shetland wool sweater out of the black laundry bag all her clothes were in. At least there was some hot water in the bathroom. Dad must have got up and put the immersion on. When she'd dressed, Rachel knocked on his door and popped her head into the room.

"Dad?"

The room was empty. Not wanting to wake Matt, she went downstairs and looked for her father. The only sign of life was the remains of the tinned supper they'd eaten before going to bed last night. Rachel panicked. Maybe the tramp had come back and taken her father away. She looked out of the kitchen window. Even in daylight, the morning mist seemed as impenetrable as the night before. Then she heard footsteps. The kitchen door opened.

"I nearly got lost out there!"

Dad was wearing the ancient Army surplus great-coat that Mum always hated, bought before their marriage. His ears were red from the cold. He was carrying a full plastic bag.

"I've been to the farm down the road. They sold me some milk and eggs, even a chicken for dinner. Ever plucked a chicken, Rachel?"

Rachel grimaced. Until Mum died she'd been a vegetarian like her. Dad smirked and pulled a frozen, shrinkwrapped chicken from the bag, followed by a large uncut loaf.

"These should be defrosted by dinner time. They tell me frozen bread makes great toast, if you manage to hack out the slices!"

Rachel smirked back.

"I think we've some sliced left from last night. Tell you what – I'll make breakfast if you light a fire."

"Done! Is your brother up?"

"No."

"Well, put the kettle on, then rouse him. I'll get the fire going."

Rachel tidied up while Dad made the fire. Somehow, he always managed to put a bright face on things, cheer her up. A week after Mum's accident he was making jokes, teasing her and Matt the way he'd always done. Dad never really talked about Mum after the funeral. Rachel threw away a sardine can. The bin was empty apart from a finished bottle of whisky. It had been half full when she went to bed.

After breakfast, Rachel sorted out her things. The wardrobe was smaller than the one she'd had in Putney. Some of her dresses would have to be left folded in a drawer. It was hard to decide which posters to put up and which to leave. At sixteen, Rachel felt too old for the pop posters she'd taken down. Eventually she settled for just one – a present from her parents last Christmas. It was a giant Andy Warhol print – Marilyn Monroe's fuzzy profile duplicated numerous times, backed on pink.

On the chest of drawers, Rachel put her favourite photo of Mum. It was taken on their summer holidays, eighteen months ago. Mum's long, straight brown hair curled in the breeze as she smiled at the camera. She looked slim and beautiful in a T-shirt and long shorts. People often said that Rachel looked like her mum in that photograph, but Rachel knew she wasn't as pretty as her.

Sometimes, in the last few months, Rachel had found herself talking to the face in the photograph, in a way she'd always been able to with Mum but never with Dad. After a while, though, she'd stopped – it just made her feel emptier inside when there was no one there to answer. She needed Mum's opinion on things. Moving to Nether Hulme might be a good thing for Dad, but was it the right move for her? Was it OK to eat meat again because, without Mum's cooking, veggie food seemed dull and monotonous? Should she have been so rude to Phil Marks when he asked her out? Would Katie find a new best friend and forget about her?

Rachel had to stop herself looking at Mum's photo. She looked out of her window instead. The fog still hadn't lifted. Last night she'd rung Gran to let her know that they'd arrived safely.

"What's the scenery like?" she'd asked.

"I don't know, Gran. It's too foggy."

Rachel looked at her clock-radio. Somehow it had got to twelve-thirty. She switched on Radio One, catching the end of the headlines on "Newsbeat".

"Dense fog continues to cover the country after the foggiest night since the war. The police report numerous pile-ups on the roads, with at least twenty people killed and many more injured. They warn people not to drive, even short distances, unless their journey is absolutely essential. It is thought that many people have not gone in to work today, preferring to extend their holiday rather than make a risky journey. Our Weather Desk says that unless the fog lifts in the next couple of hours, we could well be in for another night of even thicker fog. Stay tuned for information on road closures and a full update on the public transport situation."

Just great! Rachel thought. Dad had promised that he'd take them to Nottingham today, his last day off before starting work. Instead they'd be stuck in the cottage with just each other for company, yet again, and only the crappy black and white portable TV to watch, because Dad hadn't rented a new one yet. Matthew came into the room without knocking.

"Dad says we can't go to Nottingham unless the fog clears."

"Well, that's pretty obvious, isn't it? Stupid!"

Matthew shrugged. He had on his usual hang-dog expression.

"You want to play backgammon?"

Rachel shook her head. She only played backgammon with her brother when she was in a generous mood. He took games more seriously than her, and usually won. Matt shrugged again, and started to shuffle out.

"There's the Marx Brothers on the telly at one o'clock."

"I don't want to watch it in black and white."

"It was made in black and white. And it's got Marilyn Monroe in it."

16

Having won the discussion, Matt left.

"Close the door. And knock before you come into my room next time."

Rachel decided to go downstairs. She'd better sort out lunch before the film. She always watched films with Marilyn Monroe in them. Rachel had half a dozen videotapes full of them, but she couldn't tape this one because Dad hadn't rented a new video yet either. Life would be more bearable if she could watch *Gentlemen Prefer Blondes*, or that sad, haunting one, *The Misfits*. *Some Like It Hot* was on BBC1 tomorrow night, and she'd watch that again, even though she'd already seen it twenty-eight times.

As it turned out, she had to wait over an hour to see Marilyn in *Love Happy*, and then she was only in it for ten seconds. It was Harpo's film. Groucho hardly got to do anything, and he was the only Marx Brother who really made her laugh. He reminded Rachel of Alan Alda playing Hawkeye in the M★A★S★H series.

Matt liked Harpo. He kept giggling during the shoplifting scenes and fell about during the bits where the baddies pulled endless objects out of his huge coat – anything from tins of sardines to an artificial limb. Dad watched the film with them, and suggested a game of Trivial Pursuits when it was over. Rachel didn't want to spoil the good atmosphere, so she played. Despite her best efforts to remain aloof, she won easily.

Matt tried to get them to play another game, but failed. Instead, he started to ask about the weather.

"Why's it so foggy, Dad?"

"It's just one of those things, Matt. There's not much wind, and the temperature dropped a lot last night."

"And that makes fog?"

"Yes, if there's a lot of water vapour in the air. When it gets cold the air can't hold as much water, and condensation causes it to hang in the air as tiny droplets, which are what make up mist, or fog."

"And you need wind to get rid of it all?"

"Or a big rise in temperature. Otherwise the fog is liable to get thicker tonight. It'll be gone by tomorrow though. You hardly ever get the conditions for fog more than two nights running."

But the next day the fog was still there, deeper and seemingly thicker. When Rachel came downstairs Dad had the breakfast-time news on the telly.

"As the whole country remains covered in the thickest fog since the war, the toll of accidents on the roads continues to increase. Large numbers of people continue to ignore warnings. Over seventy people are known to have died and hundreds more are injured. Poor visibility has made recovery work near impossible. A report coming up. The message for motorists everywhere: 'Don't drive!' Meteorologists confess themselves baffled at the severity of the conditions and will not predict when the fog might clear. Many roads are closed. Emergency services report that some isolated communities are in danger of being completely cut off."

"Why didn't your lot predict this then, Dad?"

Dad ruffled his thick ginger hair.

"My lot do research, not weather forecasts. And anyway, fog's very difficult to predict. The conditions have to be quite precise, and can change very quickly."

"Well, you can't go to work while it's like this."

Dad wrinkled his nose.

"I can't drive, certainly, but I might try and get in for a couple of hours, show my face."

"But Dad, you'll get lost. I mean, you saw all the things that are happening on the news. It's serious."

"Rachel, in Britain the weather's always a serious business. But if we were in Siberia, nobody would bat an eyelid at this kind of weather. It's unusual, that's all. Now, if you're worried about being left alone when it's like this . . ."

"Oh, it's not that."

"OK. But I'm trusting you to look after Matt. You know how he gets sometimes . . ."

As if on cue, Matthew appeared at the door.

"How do I get?"

Dad smiled.

"Fed up when you're left on your own, like most of us. I was just telling your sister that I'm going to try and get into work this afternoon. OK?"

"OK."

"Right. Then get some cereal down you. I'm going to pop over to the Edwardses' farm and get directions. I'll find out about shops too, or see if I can buy some more food off them. Can't have you going hungry."

19

"Can I come?"

"No, you stay with Matt. It's a working farm. We don't want a crowd of us disturbing them."

"But if you go to the shops—"

"If there are any shops nearby open. We'll see."

Rachel nodded. She was so fed up with being stuck in the house, that just then a visit to a supermarket was her idea of heaven! Dad left. On TV they showed a picture of the Prime Minister, who was being forced to stay at his country home, "Chequers", because it was impossible to get to Downing Street. Rachel smirked: this was the first time she could remember a politician suffering as a result of bad weather. It made missing the supermarket more bearable.

"I must get to Westminster!"

Frank Jones, the Home Secretary, listened patiently at the other end of the phone.

"Prime Minister, it would look very bad if you were to travel by road after telling everyone else not to. In addition to which, the roads really are very dangerous, even with a police escort."

"You're sure there's no way I can use a helicopter?"

"The fog's over fifty metres deep at Chequers, Prime Minister, and nearer a hundred in Westminster. It's impossible."

"And there's still no sign of it clearing?"

"The Met. Office say that with the period of high pressure continuing, they can't make any firm predictions, but for it to go into a third day would be very unusual."

There was a pause.

"But not impossible?"

"Well . . ."

Frank cleared his throat. He considered telling the Prime Minister that he was over-reacting, but decided against it.

"Come on, Frank. What's the longest period of fog we've had?"

"London had four days back in '52, but back then, pollution . . ."

"That's enough. I can't stay away from Number Ten for another two days. Are there still some trains running?"

"I believe so, Prime Minister. There are delays, but on the whole the rail network is holding up well. It's getting worse all the time, of course – if this weather keeps up for another two days, there'll only be the Underground left working."

"Sort it out for me, Frank. I want a private carriage and *no publicity*. Oh, and Frank?"

"Prime Minister?"

"I'm calling a full Cabinet meeting for tomorrow morning at ten. Make it clear that if I can get there, everyone else can."

The Prime Minister hung up. Frank buzzed his Private Secretary. Let him sort out the Prime Minister's travel arrangements. Then he rang round the members of the Cabinet, politely insisting that they make a hazardous journey tonight or tomorrow morning. He knew that many would find it inconvenient, but few would dare to make excuses. At least Frank didn't have to travel – his own flat was only five minutes' walk away.

He put his feet up on the desk and, like a man without a care in the world, began to hum the tune to one of his favourite songs. The song was by the Gershwin brothers. Frank couldn't recall the words, but its title appealed to his wry sense of humour: 'A Foggy Day in London Town'.

Chapter Three

Dad came back from the phone.

"Just rang the Weather Station to let them know I was coming. They obviously weren't expecting me. Chap called Brown told me not to come in until the weather cleared. 'You don't say that to a meteorologist,' I said. Then he started going on about secret maintenance work. 'I've got Grade One security clearance,' I told him. 'What have you got?' That shut him up."

Dad put on his wellington boots. Matt looked up from the TV.

"Dad, what's the Greenhouse Effect?"

"Why do you want to know?"

"This woman on the telly says it might be the reason for the fog."

Dad smiled condescendingly.

"That's rubbish. The Greenhouse Effect is about the world getting warmer, because of carbon dioxide from all the fossil fuels we burn – in power stations and industry mainly, but also from cars and the destruction of the Amazon rainforest. All of it trapped in our atmosphere. Now that may change the weather during your lifetime, but it has nothing to do with this fog."

"That's what the other man on the telly said. But the woman says there's been all this extreme weather in the last few years that no one can explain. She says we don't understand everything about the weather."

"That's true, Matt. And part of my job is investigating how atmospheric pollution affects weather cycles. Changes are slow, but that doesn't mean they're harmless. For example, look at the way hurricanes have become stronger since the Eighties – that's a direct result of the Greenhouse Effect.

"But as for some of the extremes we've had recently – the really mild winters followed by very cold ones, the heatwaves, and now this fog – they're not so unusual in the overall scheme of things. Maybe we keep more records, pay more attention to freakish weather now. But there was a four-day fog in London as recently as 1952. It isn't that bad yet."

Rachel listened to the discussion, barely keeping track of it. Mum used to go on about pollution and holes in the ozone layer. She and Dad sometimes argued about how to deal with them, Dad accusing her of being too emotional and Mum saying he was trying to blind her with science. Rachel knew the litany of phrases she used: conserve, cut down, buy Green, recycle everything. None of them did Mum any good when she walked in front of the van. Rachel used to side with Mum, but now she agreed with Dad – damage to the environment was a trendy issue, like nuclear weapons were for a while. You couldn't do a lot about pollution, so there was no point in letting it dominate your life. Right now, she was still fed up that no shops were open. Dad had moved on to another subject:

"Another theory we're investigating is that forces outside the planet might affect our weather more than we realise. This Ministry of Defence scientist, David Harvey, is doing work with satellites . . ."

Rachel got up and poured herself some squash. There was a honking outside. Mr Edwards was giving Dad a lift as near as he could get to the Weather Station. Rachel put away some of the food Dad had brought from the Edwards.

"I should be back before it's really dark."

"OK, Dad."

Rachel gave him a peck on the cheek. Dad put on his dufflecoat, patted Matt on the shoulder, then left – a man with a job to get to.

As usual, the Prime Minister was the last to enter the Cabinet room. He nodded tersely at the assembled group of ministers, who stood awkwardly until he was in his chair. The Prime Minister was not a tall

25

man. His permanently raised chin was an attempt to command the dignity his height lacked. Yet he needn't have bothered with it; his reputation as a totally ruthless opponent scared the Cabinet much more. It is said that to know a man you should know his enemies. The Prime Minister was thought to have no friends.

Frank Jones had carefully developed his own image, that of a kindly uncle. He chose his words carefully in order to make them as reassuring as possible. "...while the situation is serious, for the majority of the public it's little more than an inconvenience. Tomorrow is Saturday. It would be unprecedented for the foggy spell to continue beyond the weekend. If it shifts on Sunday, so that we can clear the major roads, most people should be able to get to work by Monday."

The Prime Minister gave a thin smile.

"Thank you, Frank. Are there any questions?"

No one spoke. Each seemed bitter that they had been summoned, at great inconvenience during their Christmas holidays, only to find the decisions already taken. As the ministers shuffled in their seats, the Cabinet door opened. Still wearing his Burberry, John Heartstone, the Environment Minister, hurried in.

"Sorry I'm late. There was the most awful traffic jam. This damn fog!"

The Prime Minister glared at him.

"I think you've wasted your time. Our decision has already been taken. Is that agreed, ladies and gentlemen?"

None of them dissented. Heartstone sat down, flustered.

"Well, look, since we're here, could I raise this matter of the EC directives on pollution again?"

There was a collective groan.

"I don't think that this is the time..."

Heartstone interrupted the Prime Minister.

"I know, but the media are already speculating that the fog may be caused by our failure to cut pollution. An announcement after today's meeting would help public confidence..."

The Prime Minister winced.

"Or could be construed as a panic gesture."

He turned to the Home Secretary.

"Frank, would you remind us of the facts?"

Frank allowed himself a small, smug smile.

"We are committed to follow the EC directives, even though we voted against them, Prime Minister. Instead of the ten per cent cut in fumes we agreed, all the new roads we've built have led to a ten per cent increase in carbon dioxode, fifteen per cent in acid rain, thirteen per cent..."

"Yes, yes, I've read the figures. What do we propose to do?"

"The same as we have in the past, Prime Minister. Attack the way the figures are arrived at and change our own method of measuring pollution. In the Press conference, point out that all new cars now run on unleaded petrol – most people think that means they're pollution-free. And insist as usual that nothing must get in the way of the industrial regeneration of the country."

The PM nodded sagely. There was a brief pause where other members of the Cabinet could speak if they chose. Eventually, one did.

"What about the voters? Polls show that they're still quite concerned about environmental issues . . ."

The PM interrupted.

"The voters will always be more concerned about being able to get around in their cars. I think that's everything. Gentlemen . . ."

Heartstone frowned.

"Prime Minister, I must protest!"

"Not now, John. I trust you will all have a safe journey home and that it will not be necessary for us to meet again until the usual time. Good morning."

Heartstone scowled openly, but the Prime Minister had already turned away.

At five, Dad still hadn't come home. Rachel was beginning to get worried. Matt didn't say anything, but he hadn't turned a page in his *Spiderman* comic for ages.

"Maybe he's at the Edwardses' farm."

"He said he'd be back before it was dark."

"Do you want to go over there?"

"I don't know the way. We might get lost."

Rachel cursed. Her brother was such a wimp sometimes.

"All right. There's nothing else for it. I'm going to ring the Weather Station. Dad left the number somewhere."

A man called Brown answered the phone.

"I'd like to speak to Jack Gunn, please."

"I'm sorry, he's not here. The weather, you know. Can I help?"

"He's my father. Are you sure he's not there?"

There was a pause.

"Mr Gunn left a couple of hours ago. I expect he'll be home any moment."

Rachel gave a sigh of relief.

Two hours later, Dad still wasn't home.

"There's nothing for it. We have to go to the Edwardses' farm. You coming?"

Matt came. It was dark and damp. The fog hung in the air, unmoving. If Dad came round the corner now, they wouldn't be able to see him.

"I think it's up this way."

Cautiously, they felt their way along dry stone walls, up a road they'd never seen in daylight. The farmhouse was almost upon them before they noticed it, lights shining dully inside. Mr Edwards opened the door. He was a round, friendly man.

"Your father? Yes, I was just about to come and ask you the same thing. I drove him more than half way to the Station in Upper Hulme, but there was a big tree blocking the road, wall on either side – I couldn't get round it. So I told him to give me a ring when he was coming back. I'd pick him up there. He hasn't called."

Rachel was becoming more and more anxious.

"But they said he left four hours ago!"

"I think I'd better call them."

29

Mrs Edwards made them coffee while he rang. Their daughter, Joanne, a frumpy girl in her late teens, eyed Rachel curiously. Mr Edwards came back from the phone looking disturbed.

"The man I spoke to said that Mr Gunn hadn't been in today. When I started to argue with him, he hung up on me."

"But they told me . . ."

"Maybe you'd better try again."

Rachel dialled the number. It rang and rang. There was no reply. After a couple of minutes, the ringing tone turned into a high-pitched whine. The line had been disconnected. Rachel began to shake. Mr Edwards took the phone from her.

"I think I'd better call the police."

The police told him they'd try to get through to the Station. They wouldn't consider Jack Gunn missing until he'd been gone for twenty-four hours. Rachel got on the phone and tried to explain about the confusion over whether her father even got to the Station.

"Probably just an honest mistake, love. If he's not home in the morning, give us a ring and we'll have a look for him. But a lot of people get lost in this fog. He probably decided to walk all the way home and took the wrong turning. Why don't you go home now? He's probably there."

But he wasn't. Mr Edwards insisted they stay in the farmhouse that night. He had some camp beds. They left a note for Dad, just in case. Mrs Edwards cooked them a meal. Joanne tried telling them about their new school, which she used to go to. They watched *Some Like It Hot*. But neither of them could think about anything but Dad. Rachel couldn't get interested in Marilyn Monroe at all tonight, and didn't laugh once. All she wanted was for the phone to ring, for a knock on the door. Matthew didn't speak all evening. Every time there was the slightest noise, he would look up, wait a moment, then retreat into his shell. No one came. The phone didn't ring.

"Try to sleep. Things might look different in the morning."

Mrs Edwards left them with their camp beds in the warm living room. Rachel was glad not to be alone, but could think of nothing to say to her brother that would be any use. Neither of them got much sleep that night.

In the morning, the fog was still there. Mr Edwards rang the police again.

"They say they'll look when they can, send someone to the Station."

"I want to go."

He shook his head.

"There's no point at all while it's this foggy. I wouldn't have a chance of finding him, and I know the area. It's a simple enough road, but he must have strayed off it somehow . . ."

Rachel wasn't going to give in so easily. She knew what she had to do. It was easy to get Mr Edwards to talk about the road, on the pretext of trying to work out how Dad might have left it. By the time he'd finished explaining, she thought she knew the way

31

to the Weather Station.

"I'm going to go home now. Wait for Dad there."

"I think you'd be better off here."

"Suppose Dad's stranded in someone else's house and tries to ring up? I want to be there."

"I don't like to think of you on your own. Give it an hour. See if the police come up with anything."

Grumpily, Rachel agreed. Matt put the TV news on.

"As the fog covering the nation enters its fourth day, we listen to new theories about its causes, and we interview people who remember the last four-day fog, which brought London to a standstill in the fifties. But first, the latest news: virtually all major roads across the country are now closed, a result of the foggiest conditions on record in this country. The rail network is running a very limited service, as poor visibility slows trains down, leaving them in the wrong place and making scheduling impossible. Deaths caused by the severe weather now total over two hundred, with thousands more injured in road accidents. Many more people are missing, believed to be lost in the fog . . ."

Rachel shivered. Photographs flashed across the screen – a doctor, a Home Office scientist, two teachers, a firefighter, several children. Phone numbers flashed across the screen for people to ring. Would Dad be on that list by tomorrow?

No one seemed to have an explanation for the fog, or any idea when it would lift. Other countries weren't getting it, except for small bits of Ireland, Belgium and France. The conditions during the 1952 fog sounded much like this one. Temperatures stayed just above freezing the whole time. Lots of people developed pneumonia, bronchitis, and other throat complaints. Many old people died. Evidently poll- ution from coal fires made the fog worse.

The picture cut to images of the photochemical smog over Los Angeles and Santiago, mostly caused by sulphur dioxide from car exhausts. Rachel began to wonder – maybe people had pumped so much filth into the air that they'd finally done something to the atmosphere. Maybe the fog would stay forever.

She and Matthew walked back to the cottage, holding hands. Matt had hardly spoken since the previous morning. It was cold and spooky. Rachel still couldn't think of any words to comfort him. She was very scared herself.

Rachel was opening the front door when she heard a noise coming from the other side of the house – a clinking, shuffling noise. Her heart began to beat quickly. Maybe it was Dad coming – maybe he'd been lost in the fields. She told Matt to wait inside and walked slowly around the building.

"Dad, is that you?"

The back of the cottage was a mess. Rachel clambered over stones and bits of wood, trying to avoid holes in the ground. She used the building to guide her, keeping one hand on the house and scanning the ground for obstacles. Twice she stumbled. How had Dad managed to find his way? If he'd been out in the cold for twenty-four hours he must be very weak.

"Dad?"

Rachel heard the noise again – a rustling, followed by a clatter of stone. Past the house now, she nearly walked into an old beech tree that stood by the pond. She picked her way round the pond warily. It would be no joke if she fell in. Once round it, she thought she could make out a vague figure through the haze, standing by the perimeter wall.

"Dad! Dad!" she called. There was no reply.

A few steps nearer. There was no mistaking the figure, bent over the wall, unhearing. She called again and began to run.

"Dad! It's me, Rachel!"

She was within two yards of him when her right foot caught a large stone, and she found herself splayed across the ground. A hand pulled her up and the pain no longer mattered.

"Oh, Dad! I fell."

She looked up to see a wild face with penetrating blue eyes.

"I'm not your dad."

It was Stone.

Chapter Four

When Rachel woke from her faint, Stone was carrying her into the kitchen. Matthew looked on, confused.

"You had a bit of a knock. You'll be all right."

Rachel spoke angrily after he'd put her down.

"What are you doing here?"

Stone replied patiently.

"I knocked on the door before I started work. I thought happen you were all still in bed, being city people, so I just got on with it."

"What do you mean – 'work'?"

"Your Dad took me on yesterday. I asked if he had any jobs needed doing and he asked if I knew dry stone walling. Said I could start when the fog clears. But I didn't feel like waiting."

"You saw him yesterday?"

"On the road to Upper Hulme. Said he was on his way to work."

"What time?"

Stone eyed her broodily.

"I don't have a watch."

"Morning or afternoon?"

"Late morning."

It made Rachel angry that this tramp had seen her father since she had. In the light, he looked even worse than when they'd first met. His teeth were rotten and his overcoat dirty as well as ripped. He had filthy straggling hair and a greasy beard flecked with grey. He could be any age between fifty and seventy, she thought. And he smelt rotten.

"Is Jack around? I wouldn't mind a word."

"Dad isn't here. He's disappeared.'

She explained the situation. Stone listened without expression.

" . . . so they say he left the Station after a couple of hours, but no one's seen him since."

"That's funny. I was round that way most of the day."

"Why?"

"Didn't see your father, though."

"If you do . . ."

"I'll keep my eyes open."

Stone looked a little obviously in the direction of the kettle. Rachel wasn't going to make him a drink. She wanted to get going.

"Well, I guess I'll do your walling another day."

36

Because you know you won't get paid today, thought Rachel, though she said nothing as he went. Where to? She didn't care.

Rachel turned to Matthew.

"Look, Matt, I'm going out. I want you to wait at least half an hour, then go up to the Edwardses' and tell them I'll come back before dark."

"That's what Dad said," Matt whined. "I know where you're going. I'm coming too."

Rachel didn't bother to argue. She could do with the company.

"OK. Get your warmest clothes on. It'll be a long walk."

The Prime Minister studied the results of the previous night's telephone poll carefully. Public perception of his ability to handle a crisis had suffered. The opposition's percentage lead over the government was still growing. The Prime Minister was annoyed – everyone knew that the weather was not party political. Nevertheless . . . he called in Frank Jones.

"What efforts are we making to find out the source of this fog?"

"The Met. Office are working flat out, Prime Minister, but they still say it's a freak – unusually stable conditions that are bound to change at any time."

"They've been saying that for four days. What about those experimental research stations we set up with the EC money?'

Frank Jones was impressed with the PM's memory for detail. However, he had the question covered.

"The place in Scotland's not operational yet. The Derbyshire one came on to line a while ago, but I gather they've had to close it down during the bad weather. The road's blocked and their people just can't get in."

"Can't they just shift whatever's blocking it?"

"Not easy in this weather. And hardly worth it, I suspect, given the nature of the research they do. It's quite far-out stuff – satellites looking at weather on the moon. That kind of thing."

The Prime Minister shrugged.

"All right. Leave it for now. How many MPs are going to be in the emergency debate this afternoon?"

"We'll have a quorum – between sixty and a hundred. The majority are trapped in their constituencies now that the trains aren't running."

"Do we have a majority?"

"Easily. Most of our people are from the south after all. Still, I feel it would be appropriate if we had all-party support for the measures we're taking."

"You're right, of course. Arrange a meeting of the whips."

The Prime Minister expected the opposition to support him. "Her Majesty's Most Loyal Opposition": that was a farcical lie, as far as he was concerned, but no one liked to appear disloyal during a crisis. The measures he was taking would look damned stupid if the weather had cleared by Monday, when they came into effect. It was the first time the House had met on a Saturday since the Falklands war. Was he over-reacting? No. He had learned that it was always better to over-react than to appear weak.

There was a knock on the door. James Whitton, the Energy Minister, came in. His face was downcast. The Prime Minister knew what was coming.

"Power cuts?"

Whitton nodded.

"Within two days. Three at most."

Maybe they were halfway there, maybe only a third. Matt was already tired, Rachel could tell, though he hadn't said anything. It was very slow, walking when you couldn't see what was ahead. Twice she had strayed off the road and nearly fallen into a ditch at the side.

"Rachel, stop!"

She had almost walked straight into the fallen tree that was blocking the road.

"Thanks."

The tree meant that they were over half way. Mr Edwards had dropped Dad by this tree, with only a mile to walk uphill. But it was a winding road from here on. You could easily blunder off it.

The next part of the journey seemed to take forever. They walked slowly, each step a cautious one, calling Dad's name every few yards, then listening carefully for the smallest sound. But they heard nothing remotely human – only birds rustling through the trees, and the odd owl, confused as to the time of day. They found a big stone by the side of the road and Matt insisted they rest for a while.

"What will we do when we get there?"

"I don't know. Go in, I suppose."

"Will we get into trouble for being here?"

"I don't care."

"Neither do I then."

They were almost upon the Station before they realised that they were there. It was not as big as Rachel had imagined – smaller than the Met. Station where Dad had worked in London, and the one before that, in Reading. Like the Reading one, it was single-storied. On the roof was a conspicuous satellite dish. She could only see one light on, presumably by the reception area. As they got closer, she saw a door near the light, with a bell. A notice read: "All visitors report here. No entry without appointment." But there were no notices to identify the building, or its function.

"Should we ring the bell?"

Rachel paused, thinking.

"I don't know, Matt. If there's anyone here, they'll probably tell us the same as they did on the phone to try to get rid of us. Maybe we should have a look round first."

'It doesn't look as though there's much to see."

Matt was right. Heavy shades were pulled down on most of the windows, which were high above the ground. Maybe the place had closed down. Matt tugged Rachel's sleeve.

"I think I heard something over there. You're taller than me. See if you can spot anything."

Rachel could see a chink of light at the window, nothing more. Matt whispered:

"Lift me up."

Stepping on to Rachel's outstretched hands, he pulled himself up by the window ledge, on to her shoulders. He listened intently for a minute, then got down quietly.

"God, that hurt!"

"Sssh!"

They moved away from the window.

"Is there someone in there?"

"All I could see was a computer screen. But there were people moving around. I couldn't tell what they were saying, but I heard at least two voices, probably three.

"Let's look round the rest."

At the back of the station were two Mitsubishi jeeps, new models. So Matt was probably right. There were more people inside than the two who were meant to be there. But who were they? Matt frowned.

"I think you'd better ring the bell."

"Why me?"

"It's better if they don't know I'm here. I might be able to sneak in and look round while they're talking to you. Or if they do something to you, I'll be able to get help . . ."

Rachel nodded.

41

"OK. Stand well back then. Make sure you can't be seen in the fog."

She rang the bell.

It seemed an age before she heard footsteps. Finally, a light clicked on in a corridor. A bolt was lifted. The door half opened. A thin-faced, balding man looked out at her.

"Yes? What is it?"

Rachel tried to stand up to her full five foot three.

"My name's Rachel Gunn. Yesterday, I spoke to a Mr Brown who works here. My father . . ."

"I'm Brown. Your father isn't here."

Rachel took a deep breath.

"My father hasn't come home. You were the last person to see him."

"I wouldn't know about that."

"I have to get information . . ."

Rachel felt herself beginning to grovel. The little girl act wasn't cutting any ice with this man. He was about to slam the door in her face. She had to try another tack.

"The police are coming to see you. They know I'm here."

This last was a complete lie, but it might just help to protect her. The man paused, making up his mind about something. Rachel added:

"Do you think I could come in? It's very cold out here."

Reluctantly, Brown opened the door a little wider. The entrance hall wasn't very large, or warm. Brown looked down on Rachel.

"There's a policeman here already. I'll go and get him, sort this out. But you can't come in any further. This is a confidential establishment, no matter who your father is."

"OK."

"Wait there."

As soon as he was gone, Matt darted in and opened the door that Brown had gone through. Rachel looked earnestly at him.

"Are you sure?"

"I didn't trust him. Did you?"

"No."

"Wait for me just up the road when they get rid of you. If something goes wrong, meet me at the other side of the fallen tree."

"OK."

Rachel watched her brother scamper up the corridor and out of sight. She didn't like him suggesting the tree as a meeting place. That was where Dad had been supposed to go. Matt was mad, going off into the building like that. She was mad to let him go. Suppose they caught him?

A large man in a crumpled suit was coming down the corridor. He looked like a police officer, but an off-duty one. His smile was calming.

"Good afternoon, Rachel. How did you get here?"

"I walked."

"You've had a wasted trip, I'm afraid. The Station sent me down, after you and your neighbour Mr Edwards rang us yesterday."

"Oh."

So he must be a real policeman, if he knew that. But Rachel still had doubts.

"Could I see some identification, please?"

The policeman raised his eyebrows.

"Of course."

He pulled out his warrant card and flashed it at her. The photo was right, but it was the rank that intrigued her. It said Chief Constable Peters.

"Now we've established the time at which your father left this building yesterday, and we've been ringing around people who live in the vicinity to check if they've seen him. The people who work here will also get in touch with us should your father return."

"How? Their phone's disconnected."

"Well, eh . . ."

Nothing was right, Rachel realised. How had the Chief Constable got here this morning if the only road in was blocked? Why would someone so senior come to investigate her father's disappearance? She had to get away.

"Well, I'm sure you're doing all you can."

Peters smiled.

"Now, if you can find your way home, with any luck your father will be there . . ."

Suddenly, there was a commotion in the corridor behind him. Matt was running down it, pursued by three men, one of whom was Brown. Peters started to turn. Rachel pushed him, as hard as she could, getting him off balance. Matt spun through the door.

"Run, Rachel! RUN!"

Chapter Five

Rachel and Matt ran for all they were worth. The men chasing Matt had collided with the Chief Constable. She could hear them as they ran, dividing up in order to chase her and Matt. The men were bigger, faster than Rachel and her brother. Only the fog was on their side. What had Matthew seen? She overtook him and grabbed his hand. Two men were shouting at them. Perhaps they could hear their footsteps.

"We've got to hide. We'll never outrun them."

"A bit further," Matt panted. "Give them more area to search."

But the men were getting close. They had to get off the road. Suddenly there was a turning and Rachel stumbled into a verge. She lost her footing.

"The ditch here. Get in!"

They clambered on top of each other, bodies pressing hard against the cold contours of the ditch, stuck in the position where they'd landed. Rachel's back was jammed against the root of a tree. It hurt. Footsteps passed them, then stopped. She could make out voices.

"I can't hear them any more."

"They're hiding."

"Call the others. We'll take one side of the road each."

One of the voices was Stan Brown's. The second was smooth, more educated. The men shouted. The other two joined them from further up on the other side of the road. They must have been taking a path over the fields, thinking that Matt and Rachel would know about it.

"They didn't pass us."

Peters' voice intervened.

"Quieter! You two . . ."

She couldn't make out the rest. Rachel's heart was beating fast. She could feel her brother's too. She noticed that he was no longer wearing his overcoat. They lay side to side, legs tangled. Rachel's right leg was beginning to go to sleep. She whispered:

"Free your leg. In case we have to run again."

When he'd done this, she tapped her foot gently against the ground, bringing it back to life. The men were still well downhill of them.

"Did you see Dad?" Rachel had to find out.

"No."

There were voices now.

"My bloody knee!"

"Watch where you're going."

It was Brown and the other one. That was good. She assumed a policeman would be more efficient at searching for someone. They were getting closer. To the side of the ditch was a field, where the men were walking. She and Matt might have already got away across it – the men couldn't be certain that they were still here. The ditch was quite deep, making it harder for the men to see them, unless they were meticulous, but also harder for Matt and her to get out and make a run for it, should they be found. The voices got nearer.

"They could be anywhere."

"No. They're round here somewhere."

The second voice was Brown's.

"What do we do with them if we catch them?"

"Lock them up with their dad and Deakin."

Rachel's heart leapt. Dad *was* alive! She squeezed Matt's hand.

"Got enough stuff to keep them quiet?"

"I've got enough stuff to keep an army quiet."

They sat stock still. Dad was alive, sedated, a captive. It was even more important now that they get away. The next time one of the men spoke, it sounded as though he were almost on top of them.

"I say we give it five minutes, then go back to the jeep."

"Keep looking!" Brown snapped.

"All right, I ... ow!"

The man stumbled into the ditch, just ahead of them. Rachel could see him clearly – a large, short-haired man with a bald patch. To her horror, she saw that he was carrying a rifle. Rachel cowered in the ditch, praying that her black dufflecoat would camouflage her, knowing that the man had only to turn . . .

"Well, help me out then!"

Brown reached into the ditch. The other man cursed as he clambered out.

"This is useless! We can't see anything when it's like this. What'll we do if we don't find them? They could mess things up."

"I doubt it. Anyway, they won't get away. They're not local. They'll never find their way home. And if they do . . ."

The voice trailed off. Rachel shivered. Matt whispered:

"Should we go now?"

"Give it a couple of minutes."

Further up the road they heard the two pairs of men exchanging news of their lack of success. Pulling herself up by the tree trunk, Rachel slowly eased her way out of the ditch, then helped Matt up.

"We're not far from the Weather Station. We've got to get a move on."

"But if we leave the road we're bound to get lost!"

"If we stay on it, we'll get caught. Come on!"

They hurried down the road until Rachel made out a stile to the left.

"Come on. I reckon there'll be a path over this way."

They climbed the stile. Just as they were over, an engine noise approached. A jeep passed them on the road. They kept their heads down. Then another jeep came by, not on the road, but over the field to the other side of it.

"Let's get out of here!"

There was a wall between them and the road, and woodland on their side. They found a rough path on the edge of the woodland and stuck to it. If the men found them, they would have a chance of escaping through the trees.

"What did you see, Matt?"

Matt replied quickly, breathlessly, as they hurried on. It wasn't like him to say more than a couple of sentences at once, but once he'd started, he didn't seem able to stop.

"I nearly got away without being seen. I kept just behind Brown. He went into a big room with lots of computers and things in it, the one I saw through the window. I hid in an office at the side. Then Brown came past me with the other man, who was saying he'd get rid of you. I went out again and opened the door a crack. There were two men talking. They were the other two who were chasing us. One of them was saying something about a satellite, or the satellite dish, I don't know. They had their backs to me, so I put my head in a bit further. I thought, just maybe I'd see something of Dad's . . . I dunno, I should have

49

left then, hidden again, but I hadn't really learned anything."

"It's all right. You did fine."

"When I looked inside there was a fifth man, one who didn't come out after us. He had some kind of transmitter device, with a big aerial, that he was working on. Trouble was, he saw me. I kind of stared at him for a second, and he stared at me. Then he called the others. 'There's a kid here,' he said. They started coming for me. Rachel, one of them had a gun!"

Rachel put her arm around him.

"I know. The man who fell into the ditch had a gun too – a rifle. I didn't want to scare you."

"So I turned to get out, and Brown was coming back. I had to run past him. He caught my coat. That's how I lost it. I managed to struggle out of it and get back to you. I'm sorry. I should have stayed hidden. I might have found Dad."

Rachel shook her head.

"You did really well. Better than I would have done. You want to borrow my coat for a while?"

"I'm OK. But I'd feel better if we ran."

They ran.

The woodland petered out near where the road was blocked by the tree. Rachel and Matt approached the road cautiously. One of the jeeps could be parked there, waiting for them to blunder into a trap. They hadn't heard either of them coming back. But there was nothing. The other jeep must have found a path over the fields. The wall between them and the road was quite high. Rachel found the place where the tree had fallen, taking part of the wall with it. She was about to climb over when Matt pointed something out.

"Look at this stump."

"What is it?"

"The tree didn't fall over. It was chopped down."

Sure enough, when Rachel examined the end of the tree that was on the road, there was nothing rotten about it, just clean axe cuts.

"Do you think it's safe to go home on this road?"

"I don't know any other way."

Matt looked cold, weary and scared. He'd behaved so bravely that it was easy to forget he was only thirteen. Rachel took off her coat.

"Here. Put this on. You're shivering."

They continued to walk at a fast pace. Rachel checked her watch. It was two, but it already felt like night, getting colder all the time. She was wearing her white Shetland sweater and felt conspicuous, although she knew she couldn't be seen ten yards away, and she'd probably be able to hear anyone who was that near. Her dufflecoat was far too big for Matt, who was small for his age. She tried to remember how long this part of the walk had taken them before. All she remembered was that it had seemed endless.

The last part, of course, was the hardest. They decided that it was too risky to follow the Nether Hulme road until they got to the turning for the cottage. The men in the jeep might be waiting for them. So they took a footpath that was signposted for

Nether Hulme, and came in through the back of the village. They hadn't seen the village before. It was smaller than Rachel had imagined – only half a dozen houses.

"What do you think, Matt? Shall we stop at one of these and ask for help?"

"I don't know. Do you think they'll believe us?"

Dim lights shone through the windows of the nearest house. Rachel tried to imagine what kind of people might live in it. Old people, she guessed, who'd lived in the village all their lives. Would they believe a couple of southern teenagers who knocked on their door and told a tale about armed men kidnapping people at a local Weather Centre? She doubted it. But it was so cold.

"I guess they might not. But I don't want to go home. Let's go to the Edwardses'."

"OK. But have a look at our house first. We'll look stupid if Mr Edwards checks and there's nothing there."

Rachel agreed warily.

"You wait by the wall at the back. I know the way round the pond, so I can get to the front without being seen. If I'm not back in ten minutes, go to the Edwardses' house and tell them what you've seen."

Reluctantly, Matt did as he was told. They found their way on to the field beyond the cottage. Rachel climbed through a gap in the dry stone wall. She moved very slowly, knowing that the ground was covered in debris, knowing that she couldn't afford to make a sound. She reached the tree at the end of the pond and rested against it for a moment. An arm shot out from behind the tree and a hand covered her mouth.

"Don't make a sound."

The voice was Stone's.

"There's armed men at the front of the house, waiting for you. Go back the way you came. But make it quieter."

Matthew almost ran when he saw Stone behind her. They got down behind the wall. Stone spoke first.

"I spent the day looking for your father. Didn't find anything. Then I saw this jeep heading over to your place and followed them down."

Quickly, Rachel whispered what had happened to them since that morning.

"... so I guess we'll go up to the Edwardses' farm. Will you come?"

"I suppose. Farmer Edwards doesn't like me since he found me sleeping in his barn once, though."

Rachel wasn't surprised. She didn't like him either. But it was useful having Stone with them. He knew how to get along the fields to the Edwardses' farm. They approached it through the outhouses at the back. A light was on in Joanne's room, but the kitchen was dark.

"We better go round the front."

"Wait!"

Rachel stopped Matt.

"Look."

There was a wire running along the side of the

house, presumably for the telephone. It had been cut.

"Wait here."

Stone went round to the front. He returned looking grim.

"The other jeep's just up the road. Two blokes guarding the entrance. Both with guns. We can't go round the front."

"Do you think the Edwardses know what's going on?"

"I doubt it. They probably haven't even noticed that the phone's out yet."

Rachel turned to Stone.

"Can you drive?"

"I have done."

"Can you drive a Landrover?"

"I used to be in the Army. Landrovers were our main transport."

"OK. I'm going to risk something."

She picked up a twig from the ground.

"Stone, stand well back. You might scare her. Matt, be ready to run if they come round after us."

The two did as they were told. Rachel threw the twig at Joanne's window. It missed. She found another, slightly heavier. This time it hit. But there was no reaction. Maybe she wasn't in the room. Maybe she'd just left the light on. A small stone this time. It made a loud crack and the window opened.

"Rachel! We've been really worried. What are you doing?"

"Ssssh! Joanne, we're in serious trouble. Can you come down very quietly and let us in through the back?"

"Sure, but . . ."

"Quickly and quietly."

Joanne closed the window. Rachel waited, listening for a noise that indicated they'd been heard. Inside, the kitchen light came on. Joanne opened the door.

"What's going on?"

"Keep quiet. I'm not alone."

Stone and Matt followed her in. Rachel drew the kitchen curtains.

"Can you get your mum and dad?"

Mr Edwards eyed Stone distastefully while Joanne made them toast and coffee. Rachel explained what had happened.

"I don't know how much time we've got. They might get impatient and guess we're in here."

"I've a good mind to take them on."

"There's four of them with guns. It's far too risky."

"Well, what do you suggest?"

Rachel told him.

Matt borrowed an old coat of Joanne's while Mrs Edwards sorted out what little spare food there was in the house. Stone was equipped with the farmer's car coat and his low-brimmed hat. With his hair pulled back and tucked under the coat collar and the brim down, he could pass for the farmer taking a drive.

"Remember, most major roads are blocked. You can't get any distance on the A514. Head south on small roads. There's a map book in the locker next to the driver's seat. Here's the keys."

Rachel drank the last of her coffee quickly.

"What about you? Will you be all right?"

"I've got a gun. They won't think I'm here, but if they come in after Wendy and Joanne, they won't know what's hit them. I expect they'll get fed up after a while and go. When the fog clears tomorrow, I'll get out, contact the authorities, check you're all right."

Rachel saw a look in his eyes, an "I hope you're telling the truth" look. It would be hard to convince other adults, who didn't already know them, of the reality of their plight.

"Let's go."

Outside it was clear that the fog was settling in for another evening, getting thicker still. Quietly, they made their way into the garage with the plastic bag full of food, "just in case". Rachel and Matt crouched down in the back so that they couldn't be seen. Stone started the engine. It roared into life. For a moment, the Landrover didn't move. Then Stone put it into gear, switched on the headlights, and they were off.

Once she was sure they were clear of the house, Rachel asked:

"Did you see them?"

"No, but I'm sure they saw me. Check the back. Are we being followed?"

All Rachel could see was a small piece of road disappearing into the fog, nothing more.

"I don't think so. Do you know where we're going?"

Stone shook his head.

"We'll only know when we get there."

Chapter Six

The debate finished at ten in the evening. MPs leaving the House described it as a "great parliamentary occasion", but it didn't seem so to the Prime Minister. Indeed, it could hardly have gone worse. One of the opposition spokesmen was obviously either extremely well briefed, or an amateur weather expert. Live on television, he went on for nearly twenty minutes, explaining how such bizarre weather conditions could not possibly occur naturally.

" . . . either the Right Honourable Gentleman is misleading the House, or is himself being misled. I confess myself uncertain as to which possibility is the more disturbing. I put it to the House that we are being kept ignorant of a major ecological

disaster, probably brought about by this government's failure to apply even the minimal safety
standards to industry . . ."

Other Members, including some on the government
side, speculated about freak weather conditions
caused by pollution, gaps in the ozone layer and other
fashionable phenomena. When the Home Secretary
announced that the phone system was about to
collapse, there was what the BBC's political corres-
pondent described as "a sustained barracking from
all parts of the House". The Prime Minister looked
around him, jotting down disloyal names.

The Leader of the Opposition's speech was short
and to the point. She offered only qualified support.

"We will support the emergency powers proposed
today. Nothing is more important than ensuring
that the sick get treatment, and that food is
distributed equally. Like the Honourable Gentleman, I hope that these measures will not be needed
by the time they come into force.

"However, it is not good enough to say, 'We are
doing all we can.' An explanation of these conditions must be found. This government has
always had a poor record on protecting the environment. Now the whole country is paying for
that neglect. It will not be forgotten."

She sat down to a chorus of "hear hear's". In
contrast, the Prime Minister received only polite
applause from his own side. Usually, he was treated

with a respect so great that it could only be explained by their fear of him. Not today. Well, he would have his revenge once the fog was over: a couple of demotions; a few seats "disappearing" in boundary changes – they'd remember not to cross him again. But for the moment he had met his match: the fog. Were any papers able to publish the next day, there was no doubt what their editorials would say – his leadership was in danger.

Malcolm Dowling, the Prime Minister's Private Secretary, was waiting in the car going to Downing Street.

"It's bad, I'm afraid. We've kept it off the national news, but there's been widespread vandalism and looting in every major city tonight. The police can't cope. By the time the new regulations come in on Monday, there won't be much left in the shops."

The Prime Minister stared at the floor for a moment, then growled back:

"Have the army get ready to guard factories and warehouses. And set me up a broadcast for noon tomorrow . . ."

He was going to add "if the fog continues", but, looking out of the window from his snail of a car, he knew that it would.

"Why do you think the weather's like this?"

Rachel sat in the front seat next to Stone. She had to make some kind of conversation. The road ahead was empty but for the occasional wrecked car.

"It's not natural. That's all I know. Get a fog – within a day or two wind comes and blows it away. Hardly been any wind for four days now. I've never known it this still in summer, never mind winter."

The Landrover swerved slightly.

"I'm getting tired. Do you know where we are?"

"I'm not sure. I think . . ."

Rachel consulted the map, trying to work out how near they were to Derby. They'd had to make so many about turns because of blocked roads that she was no longer certain. The mileometer said they'd come thirty miles in the last few hours, but they'd be lucky if they'd actually come half that distance.

"I'm going to find somewhere to stop."

Stone found a farm track and drove off the road on to a field. He parked behind a clump of trees.

"You think they'll be looking for us, even in this?"

"You tell me, young lady. How important is your dad?"

"I don't know."

She looked in the back. Matt had already fallen asleep, despite the danger. They had blankets from the Edwardses. She covered him with one. Stone was rolling himself a cigarette. When he'd finished, he puffed at it greedily.

"First time I've driven in years. Takes it out of you."

Rachel flinched at the smell, but could hardly ask him to open a window. She looked around the back of the Landrover. The benches had been taken out. There was just room for the three of them to lie down, but the idea of sleeping next to Stone revolted her.

"About sleeping . . ."

Stone blew more smoke at her.

"You bed down with your brother. I'll lie across the front seats here when I'm ready. I'm used to less comfortable. Don't worry – I sleep light. If anyone comes, I'll wake."

"Goodnight."

Rachel didn't trust Stone, even with the new, gentler voice he was using. She thought about getting out the water bottle – she didn't have a toothbrush, but could still rinse her mouth. Rachel yawned and lay down. She was too tired. Within a minute of pulling the blanket over herself, she was asleep.

When she woke, it was morning, but little lighter than the night before. Stone was reaching over for the plastic bag with the food in it, his smelly arm brushing her leg.

"Want some?"

Rachel started to refuse, then realised that she was hungry. She hadn't eaten since the toast the previous afternoon.

"In a minute."

She shook Matthew's shoulder and he came round slowly, the way he always did, like Dad.

"Can you put the radio on? There might be some news."

Stone switched it on and fiddled with the dial. All he found was a church service. Of course, it was Sunday.

They ate peanut butter sandwiches, washed down

with orange squash. When they'd done, Stone got into the driver's seat and started the engine. As they moved forward he gave a low moan.

"What's wrong?"

"My damn ankle's sore. I'm not used to the driving."

Rachel was confused. She didn't think you got sore legs from driving.

"Have you ever done any driving, young lady?"

She shook her head.

"Well, now's your chance. We'll have to take turns. I'll show you."

Reluctantly, Rachel got out of the Landrover and walked round to the driver's seat. Why was he doing this? Of course, it was obvious. He intended to abandon them, but wasn't cruel enough to leave them in a car they couldn't drive. For all his apparent kindness, she didn't trust him.

"Okay. We're just going to drive around this field."

It was scary, circling the field when she could hardly see in front of her, but it was quite exciting too. Stone explained the controls clearly – the function of the different gear sticks, the pedals at the front – they were heavy to use, but Rachel soon got the hang of them. It was most straightforward to use the gear stick with the red knob, which had just two positions for high and low gear in four-wheel drive, except she kept slipping out of gear. The hardest thing, to her surprise, was the steering wheel. There was no power steering and, because of the big wheels, it took a lot of turning. Finally, Stone pronounced that she was ready for the road.

"Show me too!"

Matt was insistent, but Stone shook his head.

"You're too small, lad. Your feet won't touch the pedals."

The Landrover was so big and stable that Rachel felt reasonably safe. The first half hour was still really scary, especially when she had to drive off the road and over a hedge to avoid a pair of crashed cars. The ball bar at the front of the Landrover swept the hedge aside easily. She remembered Dad on Boxing Day, criticising a farmer for doing the same thing. Well, she had no choice – if they turned back every time the road was blocked, they'd never get anywhere.

"We must be near Derby by now."

"I wouldn't bet on it."

Last night they had just concentrated on getting as far away from Nether Hulme as possible. Today they had to get in touch with the authorities. So far, they hadn't found a village, never mind a phonebox. Rachel crossed a river and saw signposts for the A38. Stone smiled.

"That's a big road. Take us right into Derby, if it's open."

But both turnings of the slip roads on to the A38 were closed. Signs warned that it was illegal to try and join the road. Rachel drove on to the A50 instead, but had got scarcely half a mile when that too was blocked by a single-decker bus spread across the road. She tried to go along the side of it, but on the footpath she found a Mini that had tried to do the same thing. Obviously the driver had failed to notice a lamppost in the fog, because the car was neatly squashed between coach and post.

"Go up the hill on the side. You've got the traction to do it."

Rachel looked at the hill. It was practically a one in one slope.

"You must be kidding! You can try if you like."

"Go back then. There's a turning to a small village we passed."

Five minutes later they were in Eggington. It was bigger than it looked on the map. Next to the bus shelter, Rachel found an old-style red phonebox, which was all she needed. Matt scrambled to the front.

"Who are you going to ring?"

Rachel didn't know. There was the police, but the Chief Constable they'd been chased by might be in charge of the police round here.

"I think I'll ring Gran."

"You'll scare her."

Rachel frowned.

"Yes, but Dad's her son and she's probably already worried about where we are. She rings every Sunday morning after all. The only people likely to be at the cottage are the ones who kidnapped Dad. Anyway, she can get in touch with the police in London and explain about the Chief Constable we saw there. They'll know what to do."

Matt looked at Stone.

"What do you think?"

What did his opinion matter?

"Your sister's right. I wouldn't trust the police round here."

Yes, and they probably wouldn't trust you either, thought Rachel, with good reason. She got out and went to the phonebox. It would be good to hear Gran's voice. She picked up the phone. The line was dead.

"What are we going to do now?"

"Find another phonebox."

"That could take ages."

Rachel thought.

"You're right. We better try someone's house."

She looked at Stone.

"I think it might be easier if you stay here."

He grunted and began to roll a cigarette.

There was a bungalow with a light on just back down the road. Rachel thought about their story. Armed men running a Weather Station, kidnapping their father and trying to kidnap them – it didn't make any sense. The Edwardses believed her because they knew her. Gran would believe her too. But strangers . . . It was best to tone it down a little. She was about to knock on the door when Matt asked her:

"How did we get here?"

Rachel shrugged.

"Do I look old enough to drive?"

"Not to me, you don't."

Rachel knew he was right. She looked her age, a

bare sixteen – no older, no younger. But you looked as old as you acted.

It took a minute for the knock on the door to be answered.

"Who is it?"

The door opened to two inches of chain.

"I'm sorry to disturb you, but I'm lost and I'm having some trouble with my car. I wonder if I could use your phone."

An old man's voice snapped back:

"Phone's not working. Sorry, can't help you."

Rachel bowed her head in disappointment. Matt, however, was smiling. A woman was looking at him through a gap in the curtains.

"Let them in, Ken. They're only kids. They must be frozen."

Inside the cosy bungalow, they were made a hot drink while Rachel deflected questions about what they were doing there. She felt irrationally guilty about Stone, stuck in the Landrover with his roll-up. The man called Ken explained the situation to them.

"Phones stopped working yesterday. Same in most of the country from what it said on the news. Everything's closing down. It's a good thing we'd stocked up too much for Christmas, or there'd be nothing in the house now. Where are you trying to get to?"

"Derby. My, er . . , family live near there."

"You'll be lucky. Outer and inner ring road are both closed. And if you do get close, stay out of the town centre."

"Why?"

"There's a lot of people ran out of food already. Local radio said a big crowd smashed up the town centre last night, took everything they could lay their hands on. Police couldn't cope. May still be some of them around there."

So, even if the police were on the side of the kidnappers, they would have been too busy to look for them last night. Ken switched on the television.

"There's some kind of special broadcast on at twelve. Might say more about what's going on."

The Prime Minister's weasel face filled the screen. He looked haggard.

"This is one of the most difficult times of my premiership and I know that, for many of you, it is very painful. We are doing all we can for the old, the ill and disabled in these terrible conditions . . ."

"Horse feathers!" Ken interjected. "They're doing bugger all!"

"We all hope and pray that the fog which has covered our land for the last five days will soon clear. My government is doing everything in its power to find the cause of the fog. But believe me, no matter what you've heard, at the moment no one really knows.

"However, until the fog does clear, my government has had to bring in certain emergency measures, which were passed, with the support of all parties, in Parliament last night. Law and order must prevail, however dire the situation. From tomorrow, food distribution centres will be set up across the country. The police and armed forces will use whatever means are necessary to deter looters and others causing a civil disturbance. Only the police, armed forces and emergency services should use the roads. Anyone else driving may have their vehicle impounded and will be subject to arrest. This is for your own safety.

"The BBC network will continue to run a restricted service for as long as it can. Wherever possible, we ask you to stay at home and listen to local radio for further information. These are difficult times. The very old among you will remember the spirit of the Blitz . . ."

Ken sneered.

"I'll give him the Blitz! I don't know if he were even born then. We're being paid back for all that acid rain our power stations send over the continent. That's what this fog is."

The broadcast ended. Rachel got up to go.

Outside, Stone took over the driving, saying his leg felt better. Rachel didn't tell him about it becoming illegal to drive from Monday. That would just make it more likely for him to leave them. She explained about the blocked roads and the phones. Stone started the engine.

"We'll see where this road leads. If it's blocked too, we could be trapped."

Chapter Seven

The Prime Minister got back to Downing Street at half past twelve. He'd done all that he could, for now. What he needed was a whisky, a hot bath, and some rest. To his annoyance, he found Frank Jones waiting in the corridor. The Home Secretary looked pale and ill. The Prime Minister waited for Frank to congratulate him on the broadcast.

"Prime Minister, we must talk in private, immediately."

He nodded and, in silence, they went up to his private office. He noticed Jones trembling as they stood in the lift. How old was he? Pushing sixty. Perhaps he was getting past it.

"Well, Frank, what is it?"

"We've had a message."

"What kind of message?"

"As soon as your broadcast was over, I got a call on the secret priority line. They gave us three days."

"Who gave us three days? And for what?"

"They call themselves the National Environmental Party. They say we have no chance of working out how they're controlling the weather, and that it will get worse until we hand over power."

The Prime Minister was incredulous.

"Hand over power . . . a coup, in this day and age? Impossible. What do they really want?"

"Everything. They want us to hand over the government, armed forces, police – you name it. They claim to have support in every party, every organisation."

The Prime Minister began to sweat. The Met. Office had told him categorically – you couldn't control fog. He had considered the conspiracy theory, of course, preposterous as it was, but not on this scale.

"Who is it? The Libyans? Iran?"

The Home Secretary shook his head.

"No. I think they're mostly British. We only have one name, but it's enough. The man who called was Tom Braxton."

"The bastard!"

Tom Braxton had been sacked from his Cabinet two years earlier. Once he had been a favourite, but he had gone too far. He was in the press constantly, taking extreme positions, calling for policies too radical for any government to adopt publicly – the abolition of state education, the health service and social security. When, as Minister of Defence, he'd called for massive rearmament and the reintroduction of National Service, he'd signed his own suicide note.

"Even if he succeeded in taking over, Braxton could never hold popular support."

"Probably not. But he's got a lot of supporters. He wouldn't take the leadership himself – they'd get a figurehead. Probably someone from another party, who'd go down well with the electorate. Then they'd sell themselves as a kind of emergency coalition – saving Britain from the fog, that sort of thing."

The Prime Minister nodded. There was a gruesome logic to it.

"Why? Does he hold so strong a grudge against me?"

Jones shrugged.

"You've read his speeches. He thinks you've sold out, not gone far enough. But that's not the reason he's got support. A lot of people think you're going to lose the next election, whenever it's held. So they want to stop it taking place. A new party, claiming to be from the centre, with a ready-made environmental record, could probably win an election anyway . . ."

"But we could prove . . ."

"I wish you were right, Prime Minister, but you know how easy it is for governments to mislead the public. It would be illegal for us to reveal what really happened. And if we did try to explain, what we said would be taken as the moans of disgruntled, defeated politicians. They've got us over a barrel – either we hand over power, or, within a few days, there won't be anything left to hand over."

The Prime Minister clenched his fists.

"I'm not going without a fight. Get me the heads of MI5 and MI6."

"Already on their way."

"We'll find a way to get rid of this fog." He paused. "That is . . . you're sure they're causing it? They aren't just using the fog, bluffing us?"

The Home Secretary pointed out of the window.

"Take a look. What do you think?"

"We're stuck. We'll have to go back the way we came." The road away from Eggington led back on to the A38 and nowhere else. Police cones blocked off the entrance.

"We'll see about that."

Stone drove on to the pavement on the left, then straight across the dual carriageway, over the grass verge in the middle. They came back on to the road without even a wobble, heading south to Burton-upon-Trent. The plan now was to head for the nearest big town they could actually get into.

It was a bigger road than the last few, but they couldn't go much faster. Crashed and abandoned cars appeared every few seconds. It looked as though attempts had been made to move them to the side of the road, but the rescue services had just given up. People hadn't stopped driving, even then. A number of the crashes were head-on collisions, still in the middle of the road. For all Rachel knew, some of the cars might still have people inside.

They had to leave the road more and more frequently. In half an hour, they covered maybe two miles. When they reached the Stretton exit, Rachel said:

"Shall we get off here? The side roads before were much emptier. It's bound to get worse the nearer we get to the town."

Stone stopped and looked at the map.

"Not here. They'll have it thoroughly blocked off like the last one we tried. There's a small road in less than a mile. We'll get off there if we can."

They had gone a little way beyond the roundabout when Stone called out:

"Matt, look out the back window. I think there's something behind us."

Matt looked.

"I can't tell for sure. I think there's a shape, but then it goes again, when we go round something. If you slowed down a bit . . ."

Stone shook his head.

"Don't want to do that."

He put his foot down on the accelerator and changed gear.

"Hold on."

They were only doing twenty miles an hour, but after doing five for so long, it seemed awfully fast. Abandoned cars suddenly appeared in the front window. Stone swerved around them, scraping a couple as he passed. Finally, he found a double-decker bus parked on the right of the road. He did a U-turn, killing the headlights as he brought the Landrover to a stop. They were on the verge concealed by the bus, facing back the way they'd come.

"What are we doing?"

"Wait."

Moments later, they saw the car that had been behind them, its headlights off, going as fast as it safely could. A police car.

"Do you think . . .?"

Rachel wasn't sure what question she was asking. Stone waited until the police were well past them, then started the engine.

"Were they following us? I don't know. Would they stop us if they saw us? Of course they would – the road's closed. Why didn't they stop us earlier? That's the question. I reckon they were waiting for orders, or some back-up. They knew who we were."

Rachel shivered. Matt called from the back:

"Will they be waiting for us up the road?"

"Probably. But we won't be there."

He drove up the verge, ascending sideways to improve their grip on the grass. It felt steadier than Rachel had expected, at least until they bumped over the ditch that divided a field from the roadside. Once they were on the field, Stone turned the Landrover round.

"There should be a small road just a little ahead of us. With any luck we'll reach it before we run into the canal that's on the map."

They found the road and drove through Stretton, keeping to small roads. Matt and Rachel kept a constant lookout for police cars. Once they were well away from the A38, Stone stopped the Landrover.

"You take over from here, Rachel. My leg's tired again."

Rachel got into the driver's seat.

"Where to?"

"We can forget Burton. They'll be expecting us there. We'll just keep going south, get down what roads we can. Maybe head for a city."

Rachel put the Landrover into gear. If the police caught them, she could be done for driving under age. But that was the least of her problems.

The red light by the telephone began to flash. The Prime Minister looked at Sir Anthony Wormwood, the Head of MI5, who nodded back. Then he lifted the receiver.

"Prime Minister. This is Tom Braxton."

Braxton's voice was calm, collected.

"Hello, Tom. Frank has told me about this practical joke of yours."

"It's no joke, Prime Minister. You must understand that this is nothing personal. I hope that you will join me and serve in the new government."

"There won't be a new government, Braxton. This is a democracy. We have elections to determine that kind of thing."

Braxton laughed.

"Don't talk to me about democracy. Of course, if you want to retire, that's your decision. You're free to go where you will. We can arrange you safe passage overseas as soon as the handover is complete."

"Just supposing such a thing happened . . . do you really imagine our European and American allies would let you get away with it?"

"I think you overestimate your popularity abroad, Prime Minister. Some of my colleagues have much more moderate reputations. We have many friends there. Do you really imagine that any country would start a war to restore your government? Who would you call on? South Africa?"

It was clear that there was no point in continuing this line of discussion.

"How do I know you're not bluffing? Can you prove that you have some kind of control over the weather?"

He could almost see Braxton's oily smile as he spoke.

"Yes I can, Prime Minister. The evidence is all around you. But if you want further proof, I will arrange it for you, though it can only delay matters. There will be a slight breeze over the Western Isles tomorrow. The fog will clear for a while before settling in again by evening. Does that satisfy you?"

"It might."

Braxton's voice became more tense.

"You must agree to hand over power completely by midday on Wednesday, January the third. If you do not agree, on the evening of January the second, the weather will become much colder. We know that you cannot move your coal supplies. There will be power cuts – millions will die. Their blood will be on your hands."

"And if I still refuse?"

"By next weekend your refusal will be irrelevant. Everyone – your Cabinet included – will be begging us to take over. But I will not be able to make any guarantees about safety. Think about it."

The phone clicked dead.

"Well?"

"C-couldn't you have kept him talking a b-bit longer?"

Sir David Collins, the head of MI6, had reacquired a stammer that he thought he'd lost in his teens.

"No, damn it! I couldn't. Where was he calling from?"

"It'll take a c-couple of minutes to f-find out."

"What do you think, Anthony?"

"It's deadly serious, Prime Minister. We'll run a check on all of Braxton's contacts, known subversives, that sort of thing. But if they're establishment figures, as he suggests, it'll be hard to find them, let alone stop them."

"Are there *any* leads on how they're doing it? Frank, what about those special research stations?"

Jones shook his head.

"Both fully closed down, Prime Minister. We've got all the best meteorologists working on it here in London. The boffins' best guess is that, however they're doing it, the operation is probably being run from abroad."

"Anthony, what action will you recommend if nothing comes of the search for subversives?"

Sir Anthony looked uncomfortable.

"The most humane course would be to let them take over, Prime Minister. That's the only way we'd know exactly who's involved. Once they were in power, and the fog cleared, we'd stage a counter-attack with loyal forces, imprison the lot of them."

Frank Jones exploded.

"Good God, man! Are you serious? This is hardly the most popular of governments. If we start to use violence once they're in power, we'll be the ones with our backs against the wall. Don't you see that?"

Sir Anthony didn't reply. The Prime Minister eyed him cautiously. If the traitors had people in every camp, they would almost certainly be in the security services. Who could he trust?

Sir David looked up from the phone.

"We've t-traced the c-call as best we c-can, Prime Minister."

"And?"

"It came from somewhere in the House of Commons."

The Prime Minister put his head in his hands. Sir Anthony stood up.

"I'll arrange a search immediately."

The Prime Minister shrugged. He knew it wouldn't do any good.

"When will we know if the fog is clearing over the Western Isles?"

"By six in the morning."

He picked up the priority phone and dialled. It was a while before the call was answered.

"Ma'am? I need to speak to you on a matter of the utmost importance. Can I call on you early tomorrow morning? Thank you. Yes. Seven will be fine."

He put down the phone and stared at the wall. How do you tell the Queen that you are about to become the first Prime Minister removed by a coup?

Chapter Eight

All afternoon Rachel seemed to drive in circles.
There were fewer abandoned cars than on the main
road, but one or two could easily make a route
impassable. Driving across fields was haphazard at
best – you were never sure what was on the other side.
However, it couldn't be avoided if they were going to
get anywhere. Rachel nearly ran over several cows.
She wondered what it would be like to drive when
you could actually see.

The annoying thing was that, despite all the
danger, she actually enjoyed being in control of the
Landrover. Yet she'd never wanted to drive. There
were far too many cars on the road already, killing
people, using up energy resources, poisoning the
atmosphere. Maybe they even caused this fog. It

certainly wasn't natural.

"Watch out!"

But it was too late. Both the right-hand wheels were in a deep ditch. The Landrover dipped awkwardly. The four-wheel drive couldn't get them out. Stone started to get angry.

"You weren't looking, were you? Damn it! I shouldn't have let you drive for so long. Come on, Matt. It's lift and push time."

The two got into the ditch and did what they could. The front wheel wasn't in as deeply as the back one. They shoved earth and stones under it, trying to create something the tyre could grip.

"Try again, Rachel."

The earth and stones flew away and the Landrover's chassis bumped uncomfortably on the ground.

"Wait!"

Stone returned a couple of minutes later with half a plank of wood. She noticed that he was limping.

"Big ditch like this, farmer usually sets up a way of crossing it. This should work."

They forced the plank under the wheel, then pushed from the back. Rachel held her breath. The Landrover struggled for a moment, then pulled away. Matt and Stone got into the back and sat at the end with the doors open, shaking mud from their shoes. Mr Edwards's car coat was now covered in mud.

Matt was even dirtier.

"Sorry," Rachel said.

Stone was conciliatory.

"Couldn't be helped. You're tired. We'll call it a day here."

Rachel remembered Stone's limp and looked at his right ankle. It was misshapen.

"Is there something wrong with your right leg?"

Stone smiled ruefully.

"Something missing, more like – and bits of plastic where there should be bone, in my ankle and my foot."

"How did it happen?"

"I was on the *Tristram*."

He wasn't going to say anything else. Rachel didn't understand. Matt, however, did.

"The *Tristram*? Was that in the Falklands war?"

"Aye."

"The Argentinians blew it up just after it landed. There was no warning. I read it in a book."

Stone nodded and was quiet for a moment. Then, looking away from them, he spoke:

"They'd had us waiting around for ages. The lads had just started unloading. I was below when it started. Some of those who died might have had a chance, only the army forgot to issue us with anti-flash masks. Mind, I was one of the lucky ones. Most of my burns were only second degree. Somebody pulled me out of the wreckage and put me on a helicopter. Those boys kept flying in, through the smoke, till they got all the survivors out. I was in the hospital at San Carlos for a while. Then they sent me home and pensioned me off."

"You never saw action?"

"That was enough action for me, lad. I was in Belfast before that – another useless war. But you don't want to hear about that."

"I do."

"Well, I don't want to talk about it. Come on, let's turn in, make an early start in the morning. We've hardly come any distance today."

Rachel remembered what she had deliberately not told him.

"I should have said . . . It's illegal to drive from tomorrow. You can be arrested and they can take the Landrover. Emergency Powers Act."

"Emergency Powers, is it? They're getting worried. Well, makes little odds – we nearly got arrested today. I'd like to know what makes your dad worth all this effort. Are you sure you don't know?"

"No," said Rachel. "But I think we have to find out."

"So for your own safety, Ma'am, I think you would be best advised to leave the palace for a less accessible and more secure place."

"My place is here."

"Your Majesty . . . I have to allow for the possibility that they will succeed. We don't know how strong they are, how many traitors are supporting them. Should they take over, they could imprison you, force you to recognise their government . . ."

"You've set little store by the role of the monarchy until now, Prime Minister. If you are so unsure of your own colleagues, then the time may have come for you to step down. If you intend to stay, I suggest that you form a temporary coalition with the other parties. The conspirators would find it harder to discredit such a coalition. In the meantime, you have my support. But I stay here."

"Your Majesty . . ."

"At the very least you should give the other party leaders the information that you have just given me."

"But suppose one of them is part of the piot?"

"Really, Prime Minister! If you see treachery at every turn, surely all is already lost."

The Queen rose, indicating that the audience was at an end. She looked unflustered. Breeding, the Prime Minister supposed. Unless she was part . . . No, no, the Queen was right. He was becoming paranoid.

"We've enough petrol for between fifty and hundred miles. No more. No one's meant to be on the roads, so there won't be any garages open. We'll have to get as near as we can to a big town. Maybe Tamworth or Lichfield. Then walk it."

"To a police station?"

"Aye."

Rachel didn't feel safe yet, going to the police.

"We could always siphon off someone's petrol . . ."

The other two looked at Matt in surprise. It was

the first time he'd spoken since waking up.

"Don't you remember, Rachel? It happened to Dad once. He had a full tank one night and the next day it was empty. He said that someone must have siphoned it off in the night. 'All you need is a plastic tube,' he said."

"Well, we don't have a plastic tube."

Matt's face dropped. Stone glared at her.

"I've heard of that being done, Matt. It's worth thinking on. Mind, it only works with older cars. New ones have their petrol tanks designed so that you can't get away with it."

Rachel decided not to ask where Stone had picked up this information. They finished their breakfast of stale bread and orange squash, then set off again. The Landrover lumbered into life. At best, they got up to ten miles an hour. Even at that speed, Stone often bumped parked cars, or hit the kerb. Then he would curse the fog and revert to silence. Matt stared ahead, equally withdrawn. The quiet made the journey seem a hundred times slower than it already was.

Suddenly the vehicle juddered to a halt.

"There's a sign over there. Get out and read it."

Rachel needed to use the torch.

"We can go to Thorpe Constantine or Clifton Campville."

Stone frowned.

"I don't know either of them. I reckon we've overshot Tamworth a bit. If we're lucky, we're near the Birmingham road. If we're even luckier, it won't be blocked. Let's try Thorpe Whatsit."

But the A453 was completely closed: a huge red ROAD CLOSED sign blocked the turning at the roundabout. There was no choice but to go on wending their way through endless little villages. Stone stared doggedly ahead, but Rachel wasn't sure that he had much idea of where they were.

"Are we still heading for Tamworth?"

"I think we'll give Tamworth a miss. Head for Coventry instead. Bigger place. With luck, we've enough petrol to get us most of the way."

Rachel checked the petrol gauge. It looked awfully near empty to her. She thought she recalled Dad telling her that driving very slowly used up petrol just as quickly as driving very fast. As if to confirm this, the needle seemed to lurch backwards, hovering just above the empty mark for a couple more miles. Then, as they entered another village, it sank to "E". A warning light flashed on the dashboard. Rachel turned to Stone.

"Perhaps it would be best to stop here. We might be able to beg some petrol off somebody. Better to be stranded here than on the open road."

Stone sneered.

"The earlier we stop, the further we have to walk."

But as he spoke, the engine began to splutter.

"I think we should stop."

Stone turned round to look at Matt.

"I guess you're right, young lad."

They were by a pub, "The Red Lion". There were no lights on inside, but it had a carpark. Stone put the Landrover in the corner most remote from the road.

Rachel thought it unlikely that anyone would be looking for them there, but it couldn't hurt to be careful. Only when they got out did she realise how effective the heating had been in the Landrover. It was really chilly. As they walked through the grey mist up a steep hill, it seemed to Rachel that she had never felt so bitterly cold, and so empty inside. Her clothes were clammy and covered in grime. She was beginning to look like Stone.

They had gone about two hundred yards when she saw a sign above a semi-detached house.

"Look," she urged. "Does that say what I think it says?"

They moved closer. The sign did indeed say POLICE.

Rachel said a silent prayer of thanks to whoever might be listening. She turned to Matt and Stone.

"I'll do the talking, OK?"

Both nodded.

The man who answered the door wore jeans and shirtsleeves. He was round-faced and overweight.

"I'm looking for the police."

"Well, you've found me. It's freezing out there, lass. Come on in. Happy New Year!"

Rachel had forgotten what day it was. The constable looked warily at Stone as he trudged in behind Matt.

"I'm Constable Stokes, but you can call me Steve. Everybody does. But you're not from round here, are you?"

"No. We're not."

Rachel decided not to give him time to ask questions. She immediately launched into their story, while the others stood listening. She had had so little sleep, it was hard to get all the facts straight – Dad's disappearance, the armed men at the Research Station, being chased and stealing the Landrover.

"A Chief Constable, you say? Do you know which county?"

"No."

"And you think all this is connected to the weather we're having?"

"I don't know. It might be. Dad said they were experimenting . . ."

Rachel knew enough to know she didn't understand. Steve shook his head.

"Carry on."

At last Rachel finished. The policeman drew a deep breath and pulled himself up to his full size.

"Well, I *think* I believe you, but I doubt that them at the station will." He shook his head and paused. "Trouble is, all the phones are down and I'm off duty for two days, so I've no radio . . . Tell you what we'll do. Tamworth's impossible to get into, but there's a sub-station at Nuneaton, five miles off. I can radio Coventry from there. We could take my Cortina, but I don't fancy its chances on these roads. You say you've got a Landrover?"

"Just up the road, but there's no petrol in it."

"There's a petrol station a mile down the road. It's closed, but I can knock up Alf who runs it, get you some. In the meantime, . . . Susan?" He called to his wife, who was hovering in the hallway.

"No one'll trust this bloke as far as they can throw him looking like that. Stick him in the shower and give him some of my old clothes. Be quick, mind. I'll be back within half an hour."

Rachel expected Stone to protest, but he remained silent, and meekly allowed himself to be shepherded into the bathroom. Rachel washed as best she could over the kitchen sink. Then Susan returned and began making soup and coffee. While the kettle boiled she put the radio on.

"Are they still broadcasting?"

Susan shook her head.

"First four minutes in every hour. Long Wave only."

"Have they got any nearer to finding out what's going on?"

Susan shook her head again. The radio was silent, then suddenly crackled into life with three long pips.

"This is London. The Government has announced that this morning's lifting of the fog over the Western Isles, as mentioned in our earlier bulletins, does not indicate that the fog over the rest of the country is about to clear. We have just received the following news from Number Ten, Downing Street. The Prime Minister has invited the leaders of the three main opposition parties to join him in leading a coalition government of national unity until the end of the current crisis. All have agreed, including the Leader of the Opposition, despite many misgivings in her own party. She told her critics that 'patriotism should not be party political'. The Queen has given her blessing to this new all-party government. The new national leadership has just issued the following brief statement:

'This country is in the hour of its deepest crisis since the Second World War. We, your democratically elected representatives, are united in our determination to continue our democratic way of life in a free and proud United Kingdom, no matter what the problems we face.'

"Meanwhile, there has been no change in the freak weather conditions persisting across the country. Electricity supplies are cut off in several large areas. The Energy Ministry is urging those not affected to use as little power as possible and wrap up warmly . . .

"Do you think they know what's going on?" Matt asked Rachel.

"I don't know what's going on," Rachel replied.

"But do you think someone's using the fog to take over England?"

"And who'd want to take over this run-down little country?" Susan asked, as she left the room.

Rachel shrugged. Who indeed? And were they the same people who'd got their dad?

Susan returned with Stone, looking bewildered and uneasy in brown trousers and open-necked shirt, both of which were too big for him. Rachel realised that a lot of his previous bulk was made up by the various layers of clothing he wore. Stone's long hair and beard hung forlornly damp, wetness emphasising their length. Susan draped a towel round his neck.

"It's the scissors for you."

Rachel saw that Stone's eyes were frightened, like a caged animal's. But he let Susan cut his hair. She might have taken it all off had not Steve returned, driven by the garage owner.

"Now that looks much better. Give him a sweater too, love. We've enough petrol for your Landrover. Sorry, it's not yours, is it? Well, we'll see what they have to say about that at the Station. Let's go."

Stone towelled his hair dry with one hand and shoved soup down his throat with the other. Rachel got up reluctantly. It was hard to leave a warm and safe place. Susan kissed Steve on the cheek.

"Now don't be long. Remember you're off duty."

They set off once more into the fog.

Chapter Nine

The road to Nuneaton was one of the worst they'd travelled on, but at least Steve was able to warn them in advance of the most difficult spots. He let Stone drive.

"Though I'm not sure I should. I know you've no insurance and I'm not going to ask whether you've got a driving licence."

It seemed crazy to Rachel that the police should pay attention to such things when so much was at stake. Once the authorities took in all they had to tell them, the Weather Research Station would be surrounded, their father rescued. That was what mattered.

In the driving seat, Stone looked almost respectable. His rank smell still hung in the air, but it no longer came from him. Matt and Rachel were the dirty ones. Despite his pock-marked face, it was obvious that Stone was younger than she'd first thought – no more than forty, which was Dad's age.

"Pull up here."

There was only one officer on duty at the police station, and he listened incredulously to Steve's retelling of their story. Steve included one or two changes to make the story less bizarre. In his version, Stone had become the Edwardses' gardener and the conspirators at the Research Station were described as "Reds". At the end of it, the sergeant gave Steve the same look that Rachel had earlier received from Steve. He handed him the radio microphone.

"Here. You call this in. On your head be it."

Steve had to relay the story twice to different officers.

"Sounds like you've flipped your lid, mate."

"I do seriously think that this is worth investigating."

"OK. You'd better bring them in, then."

For the next five minutes Steve was given a detailed description of the only possible route into Coventry, which he wrote down. The sergeant looked on cynically.

"You're not taking my panda."

They agreed to go on in the Landrover.

It was only five miles from Nuneaton to Coventry, but the route they took more than doubled this. Steve connected a flashing red cone to the battery so that it was clear they were an official vehicle, permitted to be on the road. It was comforting, at least, to know that the roads they were travelling on would be clear. Rachel sat in the front, squeezed between Steve and Stone.

"You wouldn't believe how difficult it was getting across country to you. Are the roads blocked everywhere?"

"Just about. London's worst affected. If it weren't for the Underground it'd be completely choked up. The army have been trying to keep the M1 clear, so that there's a route across the country, but I don't know how much success they've had. It should be easier now they've made it illegal for people to drive."

They were almost in the city centre when there was a loud hooting from a side road. A police panda with its blue STOP light flashing pulled across the road. Stone braked sharply, stopping ten metres in front of it. It was eerie, seeing another vehicle on the road. Matt curled up tighter in the corner at the back.

"It's OK," Rachel called to him. "They've come to give us an escort."

She leant over Steve to see what was going on. Two policemen got out of the car and waved for Steve and Stone to join them. Rachel got out behind them.

"Do you know them?" Stone asked Steve.

"No. I'm not likely to, either. Look at those number plates. They're from Derbyshire, not Coventry."

The taller of the two policemen nodded at Steve.

"We've been told to take possession of your passengers."

He looked Stone up and down.

"The tramp, this is him?"

Steve frowned.

"He's the Edwardses' gardener."

"Is that what he told you?"

Halfway between the men and the Landrover, Rachel heard Matt getting out. She wanted to turn, warn him that she wasn't sure it was safe yet, but just then the smaller, bearded policeman started to lecture her.

"You're a foolish girl, aren't you? Leaving home in a stolen vehicle with a known criminal. Then spreading wild rumours about a plot to take over the weather. You know that scaremongering is a criminal offence under the Emergency Powers Act?"

Rachel shook her head. Stone looked forlorn. The taller policeman was standing over him, as if he were likely to run for it. Maybe these men were right. Maybe she and Matt had got it wrong, somehow. Behind them, through the fog, Rachel saw a small silhouette moving towards the police car. What the hell was Matt playing at? The policeman smiled at her.

"You'll be pleased to know that your father is safe at home, waiting for you. There was a misunderstanding, but it's been fully cleared up."

Rachel could see Matt's shadow peering in the police car through the open door. In the fog, though, it was hard to be certain of anything, except that these men were lying to her. She tried to look relieved. Where was Steve?

"Our reports say you have your younger brother with you."

Rachel could see Steve now, just in front of the police car. Matt was passing something to him. What was it? She knew that whether these men were real police or not, they were part of the plot. She had to play for time.

"We didn't mean to do anything wrong."

Rachel put on her little girl's voice. Now Matt was heading back to the Landrover. Steve approached from behind. Stone, unable to see what was going on behind him, looked confused by Rachel's silence. The tall policeman was getting impatient.

"Where's the boy?"

Stone spoke.

"Wee lad's in the Landrover. He's not been too well. You want to see him, I'll get him out. We don't want to cause any more trouble."

"Hold on." The tall policeman didn't want to let Stone go.

"It's all right." Steve was all smiles now. "I've got the keys."

He patted his jacket pocket, which rattled. Stone hurried to the Landrover. The two Derbyshire policemen conferred for a moment. Rachel exchanged a glance with Steve. His eyes darted towards the Landrover. Did he mean her to run for it? Rachel braced herself. Then Stone called her.

"Rachel! Matthew won't come out unless you fetch him."

Before the others had time to react, Rachel ran to

the Landrover. Stone was crouched in the driver's seat.

"Get in and start saying something loud."

Rachel shouted at Matt.

"Come on, Matt. Don't be a silly little scaredy-pants! These men are going to help us."

She could hear them approaching now. The Land-rover's engine roared into life and the vehicle began to reverse furiously. Outside there was a shout. Then Stone spun the car round in the middle of the road and they accelerated off in the direction that they had come from.

"What about Steve?"

The speedometer reached sixty. Matt replied:

"He said to try to get away. Steve should be OK. He's got a gun."

"How come?"

"It was by the dashboard of their car. I nicked it."

Matt grinned.

"I told Steve what I'd seen while they were talking to you."

"But how were you sure?"

"Steve said there was no way policemen from Derbyshire should be in Coventry. And policemen don't carry guns in this country."

Rachel leant over and kissed her brother.

"You were brilliant. I didn't know you had it in you."

Stone interrupted.

"Just look behind, Rachel. See if they're after us."

"They won't be." Matt reached into his jacket

pocket. "I got their car keys too."

"We can't be seen to give in. It would be disastrous!"

"Braxton's bluffing. I still say the problem is caused by pollution."

"Pollution poppycock! They have some kind of secret weapon!"

"People's lives are in danger. Our priority must be to save them, not to hang on to political reputations."

"So you'd give in, would you? I always said you were a whingeing . . ."

"Gentlemen, please!"

The first full meeting of the Coalition Cabinet had not taken long to become bitterly divided. The Prime Minister wasn't surprised. He had little time for his opponents. They were so hungry for power that they had seized the chance to join him in government, only to find themselves on the brink of disaster.

The two big parties had three members each, the others one apiece. From his old government, the Prime Minister had chosen Frank Jones and – reluctantly – John Heartstone, for his knowledge of environmental issues.

"We have no agreement on either of the two main options – surrender or complete refusal. Therefore I suggest that we take the compromise route – wait and see. Tell Braxton we're still considering the situation. Then we'll just have to hope that the Science people or the security services find us a solution in the next forty-eight hours. Agreed?"

There was silence, accompanied by slight nods.

"We'll meet again at ten tomorrow morning, unless there's a change in the situation."

Everyone got up to go. Frank Jones leant over to congratulate him.

"You kept them in line all right."

The Prime Minister half smiled. At least he had one firm supporter in the new government. There was a small cough. The former Leader of the Opposition had remained in the Cabinet room. She looked on edge.

"May I have a private word, Prime Minister?"

"Yes, of course. Frank, do you mind?"

The Home Secretary left.

"Well?"

"It must have occurred to you that this New Environmental Party must have a leader – someone they'll make Prime Minister."

"The thought had crossed my mind, yes."

"It can't be Braxton – he's popular with some of your voters, but not in the country as a whole. He'd never win an election or command the loyalty of the armed forces. They have to have a figurehead, someone well known, someone fairly cosy."

"Yes. MI5 are investigating all of Braxton's contacts."

His old opponent shook her head.

"No. It won't be a politician associated with Braxton. It could be someone who's just left this meeting. Or a disgruntled member of your old

Cabinet. I have to accept that it could even be one of my people."

"Or you yourself – the polls have been telling me for the last two years that you are about to replace me as Prime Minister."

"Then I hardly need to pull something like this, do I? Really, Prime Minister, I would have expected more subtlety from you, of all people."

He half smiled.

"What do you suggest we do?"

"Instead of concentrating on Braxton's known friends, put surveillance on major political figures of all parties."

The Prime Minister frowned.

"Including members of the Coalition Cabinet?"

"Yes. Don't tell anyone you're doing it. If he's not expecting to be followed, our man may just make a mistake."

"Very well, I'll do what I can. You won't be offended, I hope, if I also have someone following you. I have to appear even-handed."

"I'd prefer that you did. The whole Cabinet."

"I'll keep you informed. Until tomorrow."

When she'd gone, he called Sir David. His stammer was irritating, but he trusted him more than Sir Anthony, and this job required complete discretion. Even the Prime Minister felt uncomfortable with the situation – within hours of forming a new government, he was having all of its members spied on.

Chapter Ten

"Stone?"

Matt sat in the front now, between Rachel and the tramp.

"What is it, lad?"

"Won't you tell us your first name?"

Stone laughed, keeping his eyes on the road.

"I suppose if the police know who I am, I can tell you. It's Michael."

Rachel looked at him. During the journey he seemed to have become younger, less intimidating. But he still didn't look like a Michael.

"Mike Stone. Not quite as scary, is it, Rachel?"

She shook her head, smiling with embarrassment.

"Anything else you want to know?"

Rachel took a deep breath.

"You know that Derbyshire policeman – why did he say you're a known criminal?"

Stone grimaced.

"That's none of your business."

"I didn't mean . . . I'm sorry. I shouldn't have asked."

"Aye, you shouldn't. I've got a criminal record all right, same as most like me. Vagrancy, that was the offence. Drunk and disorderly once. But I got a conditional discharge each time, on account of my other record – the war one. Police left me alone after a while."

"Why do you . . . live like you do?"

Stone was silent for a long time. Rachel thought about changing the subject, putting the radio on, anything. Finally, he spoke.

"While I was in hospital they had this big march, see? A victory parade. Not before the Queen, mind you. It was Thatcher and her cronies. A few of us, we wanted to go along – show them what war was really like. They could hardly refuse, but they kept us out of sight – the maimed, the useless. 'Rejoice,' she said. When I got out I went back North. There were no jobs. So I drank my pension and started wandering. Haven't stopped yet. Satisfied?"

"I'm sorry."

"You didn't start the war. It wasn't worth them that died, on either side. But no one remembers them now."

And Stone was forgotten too, Rachel realised. She would never have bothered to find out who he was, if it hadn't been for the fog. She and Matt needed him. They were driving south, without definite purpose or destination. There was no way of knowing which police were on their side. On the top of the Landrover was the flashing police light – it ought to dissuade other police or the army from stopping them, but it also made the Landrover even more identifiable, if they were chased.

"I've got an idea. Steve said that they were trying to keep one lane of the M1 open, so that there'd be a route from the North to the South. Now that the roads are closed, there's a fair chance they've succeeded. If we could get on the M1, we could make it to London, get in touch with the authorities there. My gran lives in Maida Vale, and I know where some of Dad's friends live. They'd help us."

Stone considered.

"What do you think, Matthew?"

"I'd like to see my Gran."

"They're bound to stop us on the M1, even if we get to it."

"Not while we've got that flashing red light with the police logo on the roof."

Rachel smiled.

"Anyway, it's our only chance."

"You could be right."

Getting out of Coventry was the hardest part. Everywhere there was rubbish on the streets, cars overturned, shops with smashed windows and nothing left inside. Lights burned dimly inside houses, but they saw no one on the streets. After

Stone got tired, Rachel took over. She'd only been driving for a few minutes when Matt called out:

"Stop!"

She slammed on the brakes.

"I saw a shape in front of us."

They hadn't heard or felt themselves hitting anything, but Rachel couldn't be sure. She opened the window. By the side of the Landrover was a cyclist, in the process of picking himself up off the ground.

"Are you all right?"

He was a dread-locked boy, maybe fifteen years old.

"Yeah. I managed to swerve out of your way. You're not the police, are you?"

"No."

It wasn't worth beginning to explain.

"Well, I wouldn't keep going down this road. There's a big crowd trying to get into the chocolate factory – over a hundred of them. They've done in the army that were guarding it. They'd have you turned over and smashed to pieces before they found out you weren't police."

"Thanks. Do you know what roads are open and safe?"

The boy laughed and scratched his head.

"No roads are open, no roads are safe. Where are you heading?"

"The M1."

"Well, I can direct you as far as the A45, near the airport – that goes on to the M1, but it's closed."

"I'll take a chance."

Rachel found a pen and got out of the Landrover. She scribbled on the inside page of the map book. Somewhere down the street she could hear shouting. When she'd finished writing she looked at her helper's twelve-speed Raleigh.

"You cycle round in this weather?"

"Beats staying at home during the power cuts. What about you? You don't look old enough to drive that thing."

Rachel smiled.

"I'm not. Thanks."

The A45 was closed as expected. Rachel took the Landrover straight over the grass island in the middle of the roundabout, then down the verge until she found a space where they could join the road. It was worse than the A38 from Derby had been, and the long stretch before the next roundabout seemed to last forever. By her watch it took an hour.

Ten minutes later the road turned into the M45. This was even worse. Rachel found that the only safe way to get along was to drive slowly on the bank next to the motorway, hoping that she didn't run into a tree or a ditch, and trusting that the angle of the hill wouldn't suddenly become so steep that they over-balanced. By the time they reached the M1 it was night.

Stone took over. Rachel tucked his hair under Mr Edwards's coat collar. Anyone looking at them had to believe he might be a policeman. Stone's hair felt smooth after its wash that morning – much better than Rachel's did. She looked at the tramp with something approaching affection, trying to imagine someone calling him "Mike".

The middle lane of the M1 was clear, save for the occasional bit of tyre or bumper which a car had discarded while being pushed to the side. It was like driving through a wrecking yard – only the vehicles were newer and not all had been damaged, at least until they were moved. Stone drove carefully, slowly building up speed as it became apparent that the road really was clear. It was possible that cars were travelling north too. Rachel thought she heard a rumbling noise now and then, but it was impossible to see.

The Landrover was going at just over thirty when they hit the army convoy. Stone braked and tried to keep well behind them, but it was too late. The truck in front stopped altogether, and a sergeant in khaki got out. Rachel looked to each side – there was no way to turn round.

"You'll have to reverse."

Stone shook his head.

"I'm not messing with these guys."

He got out of the Landrover and waved a greeting at the soldier. Matt turned to Rachel.

"Is he going to give up?"

"I don't know."

"We could run for it."

Rachel tried to listen to what was being said. She couldn't see Stone in the fog, but she could hear an unfamiliar man's voice describing "armed looters" and Stone's quieter voice replying indistinctly. Then Stone ran back to the Landrover.

"It's OK. I used a few bits of army lingo and we hit it off. Convinced him that I was delivering some bigwig general's kids who'd got separated from their mummy."

"How far are they going?"

"There's riots in Luton. They're meant to be sorting them out. How anyone can get the energy to riot in this weather I don't know."

"Maybe they're hungry."

Rachel was hungry. All that remained in the back was some very stale bread and undiluted squash.

After a while, another truck came up behind them – Matt thought it was a tank carrier – and they were part of a convoy, doing a steady forty miles an hour. They were near Luton in no time.

"Do you mind if I put the radio on? It's nearly ten."

The reception was poor, but Rachel picked up Radio Four just as the News broadcast began.

"Fog lifted over the Western Isles today, but returned by early evening. No end to the bad weather conditions is currently being forecast. The Prime Minister has received messages of concern and offers of aid from the USA, Canada, the USSR, the EC and many Commonwealth nations. However, there is no way for food supplies to be transferred here and many people across the country are hungry tonight. For details of emergency food distribution centres and times when gas and electricity will be available, please tune to your local station or the nearest one which is operating.

"Two policemen have been found shot dead just outside Coventry. Constable Steven Stokes, aged thirty, and Sergeant Norman Taylor, forty-two, were lured to their death by three people travelling in a stolen Landrover, possibly carrying an official police light.

"Police urgently want to find these three people and their blue Landrover, registration ULH 781Y. The occupants are described as a tall, heavily bearded man, aged about forty; an attractive girl, around sixteen years old with brown hair, wearing a black dufflecoat, height about five foot three; and a small boy, aged around thirteen, with fair hair and a blue anorak.

"On no account should you approach these three, who are to be considered armed and dangerous. If you see them, contact the security forces . . ."

The item finished. At the news of Steve's death each of them had looked at the others, but there was nothing to be said. Rachel switched the radio off. She looked at the vehicles ahead and behind them. Did they have their radios on?"

"They can't have heard the news."

Stone shook his head.

"Someone in the convoy will have done, and

they'll work it out once they stop in Luton."

"What shall we do?"

Stone considered.

"We have to stay with the convoy for as long as it's on the M1. In a sense, we're protected. No one's going to look for us in the middle of this lot. But when they come off . . . we're in trouble."

The news bulletin finished. There was an eerie silence on the airwaves, then static. Rachel gazed at the truck in front. Soon there would only be the fog to protect them, hiding them from the world.

Chapter Eleven

The convoy turned off for Luton and the road in front was empty once more. Stone accelerated.

"I want to lose the lorry behind us before we get off the motorway."

"Why?"

"I don't want them able to tell the police where we got off. That way, they'll think we're nearer London then we are."

Stone took the Landrover up to fifty and lost the lorry quickly. For a couple of minutes they seemed to be safe. Then, just as they were approaching the exit, the same lorry lumbered up behind them again.

"Damn! He should know better, in weather like this."

Stone put his foot more heavily on the accelerator.

Rachel could feel the Landrover straining – it hadn't been driven this fast in a long while. The lorry was just out of sight when their exit appeared. Stone flicked off the headlights and, still at sixty miles an hour, swerved off the road at the last possible moment. The Landrover shuddered and Stone switched off the engine.

"Is something wrong?"

"Wait."

Beneath them, on the motorway, they heard the lorry go by. Stone breathed a sigh of relief.

"I had to switch the engine off because the police light's wired to the battery. It's a dead giveaway. Hold on – I'll disconnect it."

While Stone was outside, Rachel gave Matt a hug. She noticed his face was wet. Or was it hers? Somehow, Steve's death changed everything. Matt spoke:

"They can come after us with guns now, can't they? Shoot first, ask questions later, that's what they'll do. We haven't got a chance."

Stone got back into the car, shoving the wire from the light into his pocket.

"Don't talk like that, lad. Expect the worst and it'll happen. Rachel, your turn to drive. Think you can manage without lights?"

"Yes. It's easier. But where are we going?"

They shuffled about on the front seat. Stone took the place by the window.

"We're still heading for London. But first we've got to get a new car."

Matt did up Rachel's seatbelt for her.

"How do we do that?"

"Wait and see." Stone consulted the map book. "We'd better go for minor roads again. Start her up, Rachel."

The Landrover groaned back to life. Rachel drove cautiously on to the roundabout.

"Which exit shall I take?"

"Drive round them all. See which one looks clearest."

In the fog it was hard enough to make out the exits, never mind see if any of them were clear. Rachel drove straight past the first one, then slowed to a crawl for the second.

"I can see a car, I think, facing the wrong way. It might be blocked."

"Should we . . ."

"Oh God!"

The car facing the wrong way had put all its lights on. It was a police car.

"Reverse, Rachel, quickly!"

She did, but it was no use. Two more police pandas came up from behind, shutting off any possible escape. Rachel's only chance was to drive straight at them, hoping the Landrover was powerful enough to thrust the police cars aside. She didn't want to try it.

"Get out of your vehicle slowly, with your hands raised."

The voice came from a loudhailer attached to one of the pandas. Stone opened his door.

"We'd better do as they say. Wait till I'm out

112

before you come. And remember, Matthew, don't give up hope. Right?"

Matt nodded. Stone got out of the Landrover slowly. There were no gunshots. Rachel got out of her side, followed by Matt. She raised her hands until they were level with her shoulders. This was like a scene in a film, shot in slow motion. It wasn't real. From the other side of the Landrover she could hear Stone being searched. Uniformed men advanced on her and Matt, shining torches at them. There was a call from behind the Landrover.

"No gun here, I'll check inside. You search the kids."

The nearest policeman spoke in a gritty voice.

"Turn your back to us, please. Keep your hands high. Now press your arms against the side of the vehicle. That's right."

Rough hands pressed all over her body. Rachel felt violated. She squirmed.

"We don't have any gun. We didn't kill Steve Stokes. He helped us!"

The policeman's hand turned into a fist, pounding into her ribs.

"So you only killed Norman Taylor, did you?"

"No! Steve must have done that, to protect himself. Taylor was . . ."

The policeman turned Rachel round and slapped her face, hard.

"Taylor was alive two hours ago and still would be, if he hadn't come across you three. Now you're saying Stokes was a murderer. That tramp really has messed up your mind, hasn't he?"

Rachel was silent. The policeman turned to Matt.

"Well? Did you watch the tramp murder them?"

Whatever answer Matt gave would be wrong. Rachel was burning with anger now. Her ribs ached and her face still hurt.

"Haven't you forgotten something?"

"What?"

"You have the right to remain silent. You have the . . ."

"You don't have any rights under the Emergency Powers Act. Now, if you want to make it easy on yourself, you'll tell the entire truth. Who did the shooting?"

"I'm trying to tell you . . ."

"That's enough."

A new man had appeared, middle aged, dressed not in uniform, but in a smart overcoat.

"We're not to do the interrogating. I'm under orders to take them all to a secure place. You're to release them into my custody, Sergeant."

"Yes, Sir."

"Now, are you two going to come quietly, or shall I get the officer to handcuff you?"

Rachel squeezed Matt's hand.

"We'll come quietly."

They were escorted to a large, unmarked car. The middle-aged man sat between Rachel and Matt. Stone was already in the passenger seat, his head down. Another man, not wearing uniform either, was in the driver's seat.

"We're both armed, so please don't try anything."

The car started off. Rachel caught a last fleeting glimpse of the Landrover as they drove past it. She wondered if Mr Edwards would ever see it again. She wondered if anyone would ever see them again.

"Where are we going?"

"That's none of your business."

"Are you a policeman?"

"Yes."

"Then why aren't you in uniform?"

"That doesn't concern you."

Rachel leant forward.

"Stone, are you all right?"

"Aye. You?"

Stone's voice was gruff but kindly.

"One of them hit me."

"You're lucky only one did. Policemen take badly to people who kill their own."

"But we didn't . . ."

The man turned to her and smiled smugly.

"Yes, I know that."

"Then . . ."

"No more talking. We haven't far to go."

Rachel felt a cold numbness grip her body. They were in the hands of the conspirators again. This time it had to be over. They would never get to Gran, would never see Dad again. Stone had said not to give up hope, but she had to be realistic: there was none.

The car turned into a large driveway and pulled up outside what she could vaguely discern as a big detached house.

"Get out slowly, please. Stone, keep your hands behind your back." It was dark. Rachel could hardly make out anything in the fog. The house was several yards away. In front of her, the younger policeman had a gun to Stone's back. The older one walked behind her and Matt. He had his hand in his pocket. Rachel knew what that meant. She looked down at her brother and gave him a smile. Then she put out her foot and tripped him over.

"What?"

The older policeman almost stumbled into Matthew. Rachel moved quickly aside. There seemed to be gardens to the right, a wood maybe. She began to run.

"Stop or I'll shoot!"

Rachel clambered over plants and shrubs, towards the trees. Shots were fired. She kept running. More shots were fired.

The Coalition Cabinet met early. None of them had had much sleep. Sir David gave his report just before the others arrived, so the Prime Minister knew that none of them had done anything incriminating over the previous twenty-one hours. None of them had done much at all. John Heartstone went to see some environmentalists with dubious connections. This was suspicious, but he had to give Heartstone the benefit of the doubt. He was probably just looking for answers to the crisis, which was what the PM had put him in the Cabinet to do.

Sir Anthony spoke first. He took a long time to say very little. Either he was incompetent, or he was one of them. The Prime Minister decided to have him followed, too. Sir David stammered his way through Braxton's suspected associates.

"We've ac-c-counted for most of them. But, since he was Minister for Defence, you know, we'll n-never be able to work out all his army contacts. I did uncover one thing, h-however."

"Yes?"

"Just before he was r-removed from office, he had a meeting with that boffin who disappeared – David Harvey."

"We're fairly sure he's dead," John Heartstone broke in. "I had the police conduct a thorough search, as we considered he might be able to help us."

"I thought he was a crackpot anyway," said Frank Jones.

Sir David shrugged.

"You n-never know for sure."

There was an uncomfortable atmosphere in the room. All eyes kept glancing at the red telephone in front of the Prime Minister, as if they were all aware that real power lay elsewhere.

"Gentlemen, we have to complete the handover by noon tomorrow. Braxton expects a decision when he calls this morning. We can't put him off for more than a few hours."

"We must keep playing for time."

"What's the point, when we have no options anyway?"

"Perhaps we could argue terms?"

"With a traitor? Never!"

"What choice is there? We've got thousands dead or dying from hypothermia, all the roads are impassable, the hospitals can't cope, the army are complaining about having to shoot hungry people . . . We just weren't prepared for this. It's hopeless."

The last speaker was John Heartstone. The Prime Minister regarded him coldly.

"Do you have a proposal, John?"

Heartstone bowed his head.

"I wish I did, Prime Minister. I wish any of us did. I don't want to hand over power, but we can't cause more needless suffering. What do *you* propose?"

The Prime Minister closed his eyes and tried to concentrate. The dark was coming in.

Chapter Twelve

The car she had arrived in was gone. A dim light burnt in the hallway of the house where, presumably, Stone and Matt were being kept. That is, if they were still alive. Rachel was frozen to the marrow. Soon, she guessed, they would begin searching for her again. So far, they hadn't got close. Now and then she'd thought she heard something, but it was hard to be sure. A thin dawn had already passed. Each day, it seemed impossible that the fog could get thicker, but it did. Somewhere beyond it, the sun shone. It lit the rest of the world, yet here it just changed the quality of the darkness.

She'd had a lot of time to think overnight. She'd thought about whether Matt and Stone were dead, and, if they were, whether she'd be happier dead than she was here – hidden in a rotten tree trunk, covered in clammy branches. She'd thought about Dad a lot: what had happened to him; what he'd advise her to do if she could talk to him now. And she'd also been thinking about Mum. It was funny, but she'd hardly thought about Mum since the beginning of the journey – not in the grieving, empty way of the six months before. To try and keep her mind off the cold, Rachel thought about the good times she'd had with Mum, remembering all she could, always stopping short of that last tragic day. She also spent a lot of time thinking about the conservation ideas Mum used to talk about. Maybe that was a better way to remember than tearing herself up inside.

Rachel didn't really remember sleeping, but she remembered a dream. In it, a giant figure, formed out of the fog, had lifted her in one hand, Stone and Matt in the other. All she could see was the grey figure. There was nothing beyond or beside it. Suddenly, it dropped Stone and her brother. They fell, endlessly, into oblivion.

Rachel tried to call, protest, but no sounds came out. So, instead, she jumped after them. Only she must have jumped the wrong way, because she fell into the fog creature, deeper and deeper into clouds of swirling, grey mist. And then she must have woken, for she was in the tree trunk, shivering with cold, and the fog was all around her – the black, cold heart of the monster.

She had to get out of the monster. There was no point in trying to get other people to help: she'd already seen the futility of that, and she couldn't bear to see what happened to Steve happen to someone else. The only people who she trusted were inside the house in front of her. Somehow, she had to rescue them.

No one had spoken for several minutes. Frank Jones surveyed the table calmly. They had no ideas left. Even the Prime Minister seemed to have silently conceded defeat. All Jones felt was relief that it would soon be over. The handover would take place smoothly: the English prided themselves on being good losers.

The phone rang promptly at eight. The Prime Minister picked it up and speakers relayed Tom Braxton's voice around the room.

"Hello, Prime Minister. Have you reached a decision?"

"It seems we have little choice, Mister Braxton. My government will begin the handover at five this afternoon. It will therefore be complete by the time your deadline expires tomorrow."

Braxton sounded impatient.

"Why prolong the misery, Prime Minister? We could start in an hour."

"I am going by your terms, Mr Braxton. I still have some matters to deal with. I hope you will stand by your word."

"Do you wish me to organise your safe passage out of the country?"

"I will make my own arrangements. They need not concern you."

"Very well. I will call you at five."

The Prime Minister put the phone down and turned to his colleagues.

"I'm sure you all have plans to sort out, so I won't keep you any longer. We will meet again at a quarter to five. However, if any of you choose not to return, I will quite understand. Patriotism is not being questioned here: your biggest responsibility is to your wives and families. Thank you all for coming."

One by one, they left. The Prime Minister signalled Jones to stay behind.

"When Braxton calls at five, I'll tell him that we can complete the handover by midday on Wednesday. But, in fact, everyone should be able to clear out by five-thirty. Have you got somewhere to go?"

"I haven't given it a moment's thought. You?"

"I'll have to go into hiding until the fog's cleared. Then there'll be a flight to Paris. From there, straight to Washington. The Americans have made it clear that I can stay, as long as I don't make too big a fuss when they start dealing with the new British government. Do you want to come with me?"

The invitation came as a surprise. Jones was flattered. Despite their professional relationship, the two men had never been close.

"That's very kind of you, Prime Minister. As I said, I really haven't thought about it. Can I let you know at this afternoon's meeting?"

"Of course. But if you're coming, make sure you're fully packed."

Jones smiled warmly and left. The Prime Minister would go mad, cooped up in Washington. But then, he'd probably go even madder if he stayed here.

There were two cars outside the house – a Mercedes and a Jaguar. She tried the Jaguar first: it was locked. The Mercedes, however, was open. Stone had hinted that he knew how to steal a car, but she didn't have Stone any more. Maybe she could steal the keys. Rachel tried every downstairs window and both of the doors. They were all locked and burglar-alarmed. Her chances of getting in were nil. Soon, more men would come. They would not expect her to have returned so close to the house, but eventually, they would find her, or she would die of cold. Rachel waited.

A light came on in the hallway. The front door opened. Two men came out. One carried a shotgun. The other was talking.

" . . . are all being watched. Police are keeping a man in all the nearby villages as well as the ones who are waiting at the bottom of the drive. Don't worry: she won't get away."

"It's damned embarrassing, Tom. If she's caught, our boys'll have to give the same sort of explanations again: why she shouldn't be questioned; why we only want certain policemen involved. And we have to keep the other two alive, just in case some keen PC shows up with Goldilocks and want to reunite her with the two bears."

"You're over-reacting. It'll all be over by this afternoon. Best bet is the girl will die of exposure and won't be found until the fog lifts. But there's just the chance that she's still somewhere on the estate, ready to make trouble. That's a risk we can't afford. The search party will make sure."

Rachel pressed herself against the wall of the house. They were halfway down the drive now. She picked out the words "search party" again and "dogs". Then the man carrying the gun said "damn" and began to run back to the house. She was near the front door: if his eyesight was good he'd see her at any moment. She froze to the wall. He came within a metre of her. But the man was in a hurry. He fumbled his key in the lock and swung the door open, not closing it behind him. Then he went across the hallway, into a room off the side.

Praying that the other man, the one called Tom, wouldn't be able to see her from where he was standing, Rachel slid into the hallway. It was very large and very bright. She could hear the man coming back. In a panic, she opened the first door she saw and stepped into it: a toilet.

From the hallway, she heard a voice saying:

"This is the General. Circumstances force both of us to leave the house for a brief period. There is no cause for alarm. Leave a message after the tone."

A moment later, the door slammed. Rachel vomited violently into the bowl.

When she'd finished being sick, Rachel went back into the hall to look for Stone and Matt. On the floor was some kind of radio transmitter, with an answering machine attached to it. She passed it and tried a door. The kitchen. In the fridge there was some apple juice. She drank it straight from the carton to wash away the sick taste. Then she looked in drawers until she found a sharp knife. Hopefully, they were tied up, not handcuffed. Hopefully, the men had seen no need to lock the room they were kept in.

Matt and Stone weren't anywhere on the ground floor. Rachel climbed the stairs, passing a portrait of a man in uniform – the man she'd just heard describe himself as "the General". The first room she tried was massive: it had a huge table surrounded by chairs and a white noticeboard. There was a map of Britain, with dark blue counters all over it – the largest numbers in the South and Midlands; fewer in the North and Wales; hardly any in Scotland. Rachel noticed that there was a name card in front of each chair. One was for a General Sanders, another for a Tom Braxton. The card at the head of the table was for a familiar name. Rachel was sure he was important in the government. But it was clear that this would soon be the new government; perhaps, as the man called Tom had said, by this afternoon. She switched off the light and hurried out.

In an increasing panic, Rachel opened door after door, praying that no one outside could see the lights she switched on. She almost missed the closet next to the master bedroom. Stone and Matt almost filled it, sitting back-to-back on two chairs tied together. Rachel switched on the light and cut the gag from Matt's mouth.

"Rachel! How . . .?"

"No time to explain now. I've got to free Stone first, see if he can steal a car."

Matt nodded. Rachel talked as she cut the ropes holding Stone, explaining what the General and Braxton were doing and where the car was.

"We have to hurry. Once they realise we're away again, half the police force will be after us, but until then they're only looking for one girl on foot. Can you steal the car?"

Stone reached into his pocket and removed the wire he'd taken from the police light.

"I learnt some odd things in the army. Join me outside."

While Stone went off, Rachel cut Matt free.

"It's them, isn't it, Rachel? The ones who were holding us are the people who are controlling the weather."

"Yes. And by evening this house will be full of the whole lot of them, whoever they all are. We've got to get away fast." They ran down the stairs. Matt pointed at the transmitter in the hall.

"That's like the one at the Weather Station."

"Yes. It would be. I'll explain later. Come on!"

"Wait."

A light was flashing on the transmitter. Matt reached over and flicked a switch.

"Come on! They'll get us."

The General's voice came from the answering machine, then the tone. The voice that spoke next was instantly familiar, a politician – it could even be the one whose name she'd seen at the head of the table upstairs.

"This is to confirm that the PM is preparing to resign, unless he comes up with a new tactic in the next few hours. I think he suspects that our friend is not reliable, but it's too late for that information to be of any use to him. Over and out."

"Matt, I think that was . . ."

"Never mind. Come on, Rachel – help me lift this. We've got to smash it up."

The radio transmitter wasn't too heavy. They threw it at the ground. It made a crunching noise. Plastic display panels cracked. Then Matt jumped on it for good measure. The aerial broke off. That would slow them down.

Stone had got the engine going. Rachel and Matt got into the car.

"What the hell have you been doing? They'll be back any minute."

"I'll tell you as we drive. Let's go."

Chapter Thirteen

The Mercedes was more comfortable than the Landrover, but Rachel felt less safe in it. They rejoined the
Ml. Stone drove as fast as he dared. There was
nothing else on the road.

"I reckon we've got half an hour in this car before
all hell breaks loose. With no phone and no radio it'll
take them a while to make contact, but then they'll
have all the army and police on to us."

Matt sat in the back with Rachel.

"But we're still going to our Gran's, aren't we?"

Stone was silent. Rachel thought it over.

"We need to be able to hide with someone we trust,
someone who'll believe us and be believed. It has to
be Gran."

The motorway was empty. In a way, Rachel

wished that she was driving. Concentrating on the road would give her less time to think, less time to contemplate how much danger they were in. She wished she'd taken the tape out of the answering machine. It would have been a kind of proof; should they find some trustworthy police. But they'd been in too much of a hurry. All those people after them. The road was quiet. Too quiet.

They were at the end of the motorway. Stone talked to them in the back.

"I know where to go. I've hitched from here often enough. Hendon Central tube."

The Mercedes wasn't as flexible as the Landrover though, and they had to abandon it just after Brent Cross Shopping Centre. Stone made them get out, then drove the car into the middle of the road where two buses had collided, one toppling over. He put the car between them.

"It won't be as easily noticed there."

The road was deserted. No lights shone in the gutted shopping centre. It was half an hour before they reached Hendon itself. Rubbish covered the streets, and most shop windows were smashed, with nothing inside but more debris. Rachel noticed a poster that had been pasted on one window which was still intact: THE FOG IS OUR FAULT! STOP POLLUTION! PROTECT THE PLANET! THINK GLOBALLY – ACT LOCALLY! DEMONSTRATE! The details of where to demonstrate had been roughly torn off. Rachel hurried on to keep up with the others. It was eerily silent. After a few hundred yards, however, they began to hear footsteps. Without street lamps, it was as though ghosts were walking by.

The number of footsteps increased. When they got to the station, it was clear why so many people were hurrying. A notice announced that the only train of the morning left in two minutes. Stone paid for the tickets. No one gave him a second glance. They weren't the only scruffy ones there.

On the platform, Rachel had a shock. There were only about thirty people, but that was twenty-odd more than she'd seen at any time in the last seven days. Some were making a pretence of normality, with suits and briefcases. Maybe they worked for a government department that was still running. Others looked like they'd been sleeping on the streets. Litter covered the platform. Matt picked up a newspaper and Rachel told him to put it back.

"It'll be ancient. They haven't been published for days."

"I know, but . . . look. I recognise that man."

Rachel and Stone looked over his shoulder. The paper was dated December 27th, five days ago. The photograph was of a youngish, bespectacled man called David Harvey. It was one of a group of photographs showing people who'd disappeared in the previous night's fog.

"He was the man in the Weather Station. The one with the transmitter. I'm sure. And he's a scientist. Dad told me about him – he does weather research. He must be the one controlling it!"

"Ssssh."

Rachel panicked. Everyone seemed to be looking in their direction. Then she realised the reason. A train was coming in. They got on and made for a corner of the carriage, trying to keep away from the others. Rachel looked out of the window. She didn't know what she feared most – the police, the army, or Braxton. The train started off.

The threat, when it came, was from much nearer. Rachel noticed a middle-aged man in a pin-striped suit who was looking at them suspiciously. Had he heard the radio bulletins about a bearded man with a teenage boy and girl? She felt his inquiring gaze like a knife. If he had heard the phrase "to be considered armed and dangerous", he might keep away. But should a policeman appear . . .

The first few stations passed without incident, familiar names of places she'd never actually been – Golders Green, Hampstead, Chalk Farm. The carriage filled up. Rachel could still feel the man looking at her, but she didn't look up, except when they were in a station. At Camden Town, there were police on the platform. A pair of them got on at the other end of their carriage. Rachel realised that police were getting in at every carriage. They must have found the Mercedes. It was over.

Two policemen were slowly making their way along the carriage. A large skinhead blocked her view, but Rachel could sense them coming. The next stop was Mornington Crescent, less than a minute away. If only . . . she glanced again at the map above the seats and realised that the train they were on didn't go through there. The middle-aged man in the pin-stripes was giving her an even more suspicious look. He reached over to Stone.

"Excuse me!"

Stone coughed.

"Yes?"

"Your daughter doesn't look very well. Would she like a barley sugar?"

"That's very kind of you."

Stone took the crumpled paper bag and passed it to Rachel, who smiled nervously at the man. She hadn't eaten for twenty-four hours, but hunger was the last thing on her mind now. Matt, however, was looking at the bag enviously. The man smiled at him.

"Please take one."

Rachel removed the cellophane and put the yellow sweet into her mouth. The sugar tasted good. Matt was passing the bag back when the youth with the denim jacket and a skinhead haircut grabbed it from him.

"Fair shares, mate! I haven't eaten today!"

"Hey! That's mine."

The train was pulling into Euston. The man in the pin-stripes stood up, appealing to the other passengers rather than to the youth himself.

"He took my sweets – my last few."

Everyone ignored him, including, shame-faced, Rachel, Matt and Stone. The youth got out of the carriage and began to walk away. The sweet man shouted to the policemen, who were just about to push past him and the other standing commuters, into Rachel's section of the carriage.

"He's a thief. Go on! Stop him!"

Rachel couldn't stop herself looking. The man's face was red. Instead of pushing, the policemen were being pushed back. Reluctantly, they got out of the carriage with the man and started after the youth. Rachel looked out of the window. Police were getting out of every carriage. As they did they noticed the policemen chasing the youth, and began to run after them. The youth looked back to see a dozen police following him. As their train moved off, Rachel saw him throwing a handful of barley sugars at their feet.

Matt and Rachel began to giggle. Everyone else on the carriage was quiet, avoiding each other's eyes. Rachel hugged her brother, then looked at Stone. He was smiling too. She put her arm round his shoulder and kissed him on the cheek.

"We're going to make it!"

"One step at a time, Rachel. That's all I've learned in this life – take each moment as it comes."

He whispered into her ear.

"At St Pancras, we'll split up. When the train comes, we should each get in separate carriage. Right?"

"I'm not leaving Matt on his own."

"That's up to you. But stay away from me. I'm the one they'll be looking for most."

The train pulled into St Pancras and emptied. Only as they stepped on to the platform did Rachel realise that the station was swarming with police.

Frank Jones got off the Metropolitan line at White City and hung around the Gents long enough to be sure no one was following him. The tube was so crowded that it was easy for anyone to travel incognito – even a member of the Coalition Government – but Jones was a cautious man. He put the collar of his mac up and merged with the fog.

The BBC's White City studios were practically deserted, but he had a key. The senior figure who greeted him was one he'd appointed.

"You're quite sure of everyone involved with this recording?"

"Quite sure, Frank. They're with us. I'd trust them with my life."

"That's what you're doing."

The set in the small studio was made up to look like 10 Downing Street. Jones sat down in the leather chair and read over his text while the girl put on make-up. The bright studio lights were switched on.

"Whenever you're ready, sir."

The red light shone. Frank Jones composed himself, then smiled reassuringly.

"Good evening. The last seven days have been the most testing time for the British people since the Second World War. As a member of the Coalition Government, I have been moved by the common-sense and decent behaviour of the vast majority of the British people."

He paused and looked more serious.

"However, I have been deeply disturbed by what I have seen in the new government. The members of the coalition have long known the cause of the fog covering our country, and have the scientific means to get rid of it. But they have chosen not to. Why? For two reasons – first, to preserve their own influence. They did not care how many people died as long as they held on to the scraps of power. Secondly, because shifting the fog is expensive. These awful weather conditions are the result of our destroying the environment with pollution – cleaning it up won't be cheap. They didn't want to spend the money.

"So, most reluctantly, I have joined forces with a number of like-minded colleagues from all political parties and all walks of life. We have taken over the government in order to save the country. I can now tell you that, tomorrow morning, the fog will begin to clear."

Jones waited a moment for this information to sink in.

"My colleagues and I intend to call ourselves the New Environmental Party, and will restore full democracy as soon as possible. In the meantime, movement about the country will still be restricted, other than for employment purposes. The media will also work under certain constraints, so that we can ensure a quick return to normality. Now is a time to rejoice. God save the Queen! God keep our land green!"

The Home Secretary let his syrupy smile linger for the cameras, then turned to the BBC executive.

"How was that? Do you want another take?"

"Just the right blend of touch and tender. Loved the ending."

Frank Jones got up to go.

"If all goes well, we should be able to put that out on the midday broadcast tomorrow. The PM may want to record a broadcast before he goes. If he does, tape it, but put out mine instead."

He left White City, heading straight back to Downing Street and the Prime Minister, whistling as he waited for his train.

Chapter Fourteen

Rachel pushed through the passage leading to the Circle Line. Matt walked just behind her. Stone was several paces ahead of them, darting between people, keeping his head down. They avoided eye contact with the police, who were everywhere. This was hard, because the station was busy, but still a lot quieter than usual. It felt strange. Not just because of the police, or the rubbish all over the place, Rachel realised – but because there were no tourists, just plenty of ordinary Londoners who still had some kind of reason for moving around.

They reached their platform. Rachel stood with her back to the line and stared at a peeling film poster. The "next train" sign said three minutes. Matt shuffled his feet, still sucking his barley sugar. Eating the sweet had made Rachel realise just how hungry she was. She glanced down the platform, looking for Stone. At first she missed him. He was standing among a group of workmen, successfully trying to be inconspicuous.

Rachel tried to work out what to do, when and if they got to Gran's. If she was right, and the man whose voice she'd heard on the transmitter was Frank Jones, the politician, then things were really serious. Jones used to be Home Secretary and, she'd heard on the news, was now in the Coalition Cabinet. Who could she expose him to? If someone that powerful was a traitor, who could she possibly trust?

The "next train" sign changed to two minutes. Rachel watched Stone. He had both hands in his pockets and was staring at the tube line, as though contemplating throwing himself under the oncoming train. The men around him had shifted slightly – she could see his face. He looked peaceful: nowhere near as tense as she felt. "Living in the moment", she thought. It must take a lot of practice.

Next to Rachel, Matt shuffled uncomfortably. She put a hand on his shoulder to calm him, and began to gaze at the "next train" sign. From the corner of her eye she saw Stone also look up, sneaking a glimpse of the illuminated notice. After an agonising interval, it changed to one minute.

Suddenly, four policemen swept down the platform from Stone's end. Stone wasn't looking in Rachel's direction. She couldn't alert him. One of the policemen pointed at Stone and she backed away, grabbing hold of her brother and preparing to run. The people around her, seeing the police, watched and pointed.

"Why doesn't he run?" Matt asked Rachel.

"He doesn't know they've spotted him."

One of the policemen tapped Stone on the shoulder. Stone turned and smiled. He was going to try and bluff him, the way he had the army sergeant on the M1. But this man knew who he was – a kidnapper, at the very least. Stone moved away from the group of people he'd been standing with. The other policemen were looking round, trying to see her and Matt. Rachel turned, her eyes searching for an escape route. At the other end of the platform was another group of police, approaching fast. All three of them were going to be captured.

Stone was being marched towards them. There was nowhere for him to run. The only possible escape route was just in front of her and Matt, the passage leading back towards the Northern line. For a split second, Rachel thought she saw Stone look at her and smile. Then he broke into a run.

Stone turned into the passage and out of sight. The police were right behind him. Even with two good legs, he'd have had no chance. The other group of police, who had been behind Matt and Rachel, now ran past them, into the passageway. People crowded around the entrance, looking to see what was happening. Rachel and Matt hung back.

Two gunshots sounded.

Beneath the screaming and the sound of her own

sobbing, Rachel half heard the train coming in. Matt pulled her by the hand and they got on to it. Her brother dragged her to a seat at the farthest end, where she sat, weeping. A moment later, other people started getting on to the train, their normal London reticence forgotten in the shocking events. Rachel seemed to hear every word.

"Just shot him. What do you think he was, a looter?"

"They could have caught him. Didn't need to do that."

"Dead? I'd say so. Did you see him on the ground?"

"Looked like a dosser to me. The only thing that'll miss him is his cardboard box."

"I don't care who he was. It was still cold-blooded murder."

None of them really took in the teenage girl huddled up next to her brother, who stayed on the train until Paddington. If they did, all they saw was a girl who'd been frightened by gunshots, crying her eyes out.

Chapter Fifteen

Frank Jones was on the phone.

"Shot dead? That's good work. No, don't worry, there won't be any recriminations. Promise your men that. What about the girl and boy? Do you know where they're likely to be going? All right, take them there. But listen, I don't want them interrogated. That's right. They have important information, but they're likely to be muddled. I want you to take them into custody. Sir Anthony and . . . no, better forget Sir Anthony. No one but me is to talk to them. Got that? *No one*."

He put down the phone and allowed himself a Cheshire Cat smile. The Prime Minister walked into his office.

"Any news?"

Frank shook his head.

"We've done our best to trace Braxton, but all we've found out is what we already guessed. Braxton's contacting us using a radio transmitter, patched through the security phone network in the Commons. We can try to get a better fix when he next calls, but by then it will be too late."

The Prime Minister nodded.

Sir David appeared at the door, looking flushed.

"You were right, P-Prime Minister. The old man's g-given the game away. Our surveillance officer overheard him trying to radio Braxton!" Jones looked up at the Intelligence Chief.

"Who are you talking about? Sir Anthony?"

The Prime Minister interrupted before Sir David could reply.

"*You* suspected Sir Anthony?"

Jones hardly hesitated.

"I was beginning to think that there must be a traitor somewhere high up in security. That meant it was either Wormwood . . . or David."

He looked apologetically at the Head of MI6.

The Prime Minister nodded his head impatiently.

"I want Sir Anthony arrested and interrogated as soon as possible. Frank, would you supervise the operation?"

"Of course."

"Right. Come on, David. I want your full report."

Sir David started. Jones lingered for a moment, then left. When he'd gone, the Prime Minister interrupted the report:

"Have you had Frank Jones followed, as I requested?"

"All of the C-coalition C-cabinet, yes."

"Anything unusual?"

"Well, he went to the BBC this morning – couldn't ask him why, obviously. Presumably visiting a f-friend. Hardly unusual though. As Home Secretary, he was in charge of the BBC, after all."

"See if you can find out what he was doing there. It's just . . . I overheard him on the phone as I came in – there was something in his voice, I can't explain it. Do you know anything about two children and a tramp being chased by the police?"

Sir David shook his head.

"Not my p-province. I heard something on the news. Two policemen were m-murdered, so I suppose Jones has an interest in it."

"Yes, but he was gloating over the fact that this man had been shot, and insisting on interrogating the children himself. Doesn't that strike you as unusual?"

"Unheard of."

"That's what I thought. Now, while Jones is out of the way dealing with Sir Anthony, I'd like you to find out what's going on with these children. Talk to them yourself."

Sir David frowned.

"Jones was in charge of the p-police. You can override his orders, but if he is the t-traitor, some of them are p-probably in with him."

"That's a risk we have to take. We must try to get to them first."

The Prime Minister looked at his watch. They had four hours.

There were no police at Paddington, but they had a long wait for their final tube, to Maida Vale. Rachel was tempted to get out of the Underground system and walk, but she wasn't sure of the way, even without the fog.

"Do you think they'll shoot us, too, Rachel?"

"If they catch us, they might."

"They can't all be bad."

"No. But we can't know which are and which aren't. And soon it'll be too late. I heard Tom Braxton telling the General outside the house – they're going to take over this afternoon."

"It's not too late. If Gran knows somebody who can get a message to someone . . . there might be a policeman she can trust. If only . . ."

The train came in. It was a short journey. Matt kept talking and Rachel let him. He'd been quiet for so many months. Now she knew that he was talking about these things because it was the only way he had of shutting out even darker thoughts.

"If they do take over, do you think they'll set Dad free?"

"Maybe. But he might know too much."

Like us, she could have said.

"But if he promised to keep quiet, and we did too, things might be all right. They'll get rid of the fog . . ."

"And the government."

"Yeah, but the government doesn't make much difference to anything, does it?"

"I don't know."

The tube pulled into Maida Vale. Matt started to get up. Rachel looked out of the window. It was only a shadow, but . . . she grabbed Matt's wrist.

"Wait. We'll get off at the next one."

"Why?"

"They might have worked out where we're going. They might be waiting." Beads of sweat dropped from her brother's face. The train started up again. Rachel's mind cut out. When, a moment later, Matt shook her arm, she woke from a frightening emptiness.

"This is it then. Kilburn Park."

There were no police waiting at the station, or on the street outside. Matt and Rachel walked down Kilburn High Street hand in hand, crunching over broken glass and endless rubbish. When the weather changes, she thought, and the wind blows the fog away, people will see this mess. And some of it will blow into their faces. Everything smelt rotten – worse than her and Matt, far worse than Stone when they first met him.

She remembered shopping on this road with Mum, just before she died, getting a present to take to Gran's. What had it been? She couldn't remember. All she remembered was chatting with Mum, about the future. All those plans! Rachel was luckier than Matt, she realised. She'd had three more years of life with their mother. Three years of a more mature relationship. It wasn't fair on him.

Kilburn High Street became Maida Vale Road. They were nearly at Gran's now. Even in the fog, she recognised every building, every street name.

"Do you think she'll be in, Rachel?"

"Where else would she be?"

"Do you remember those breakfasts she makes? With sausage and egg and bacon, and black pudding, and mushrooms and tomato if you want, and fried bread and . . ."

"Don't."

It had only been last week. Dad's favourite breakfast on Christmas Day. He hadn't even finished it. Now she was very, very hungry. Only a hundred yards to go. Rachel felt faint and swayed into her brother.

"Come on. We're nearly there."

She smiled weakly.

"You've grown up, this last week."

Matt's face was pale.

"I didn't want to grow up."

A big van was right across Gran's road. Rachel looked cautiously before walking round the back of it. The road was quiet. Outside Gran's flat, the rubbish was stacked neatly, not like all the others. A light was on in her living room window . . .

"That's them!"

Two policemen were running from the other end of the street. Rachel turned back. She didn't have the strength to run. But Matt did. He charged back the way they'd come, straight into the arms of the police who were getting out of the back of the van. A policewoman grabbed her. "I will not faint," she said to herself, "I will not give them the satisfaction of seeing me faint." Another police car pulled up. The police seemed to be everywhere. Why did they need so many?

"Come on, Rachel."

The policewoman spoke to her as though she were a naughty child. "There's someone very important who wants to see you."

Chapter Sixteen

Each member of the Cabinet sat quietly, resigned to his own fate. The Prime Minister was late, but that was his prerogative. John Heartstone turned to Frank Jones.

"You haven't heard anything?"

"I'm afraid not."

"Where are you going after this?"

"I've made plans. You?"

"My wife's with her parents in Cheam. I'll join her there. See what happens."

The Prime Minister came in, accompanied by Sir David. He didn't look as ravaged as he had in the last forty-eight hours, Jones noticed. He looked like a man who was resigned to his fate: a man who had finally shed the burdens of office.

Even his voice was mellower.

"Gentlemen. I haven't asked Sir Anthony to join us. This morning an MI6 surveillance team heard him attempting to radio a message to Tom Braxton. He didn't get through, but unfortunately we didn't get him either. We followed him to see if he'd lead us to some of the other plotters, and he got away."

Jones broke in.

"My fault, I'm afraid. David wanted to take him straight away, but I took a gamble. It didn't pay off."

Sir David was conciliatory. "It made no difference. Anthony was a professional. He wouldn't have broken under interrogation. There is one thing I want to tell you, Frank. About those children who were kidnapped..."

Jones's expression didn't change.

"Oh yes?"

"Well, as you know, the police shot the tramp who'd taken them, as I believe you ordered them to."

"Examples have to be set at a time like this."

Sir David smiled. Jones noticed that his stammer had disappeared.

"Of course. Evidently you asked that the children be picked up and brought straight to you."

"That's right. I thought it just possible that there was some tie in with the fog business. A guess, that's all but ... any port in a storm."

Jones glanced over at the Prime Minister's face. He appeared to be taking him at his word.

"Well, it was a good guess, Frank. The children

were picked up, as you ordered. There was a bit of confusion, actually, but they found their way to me three hours ago. They had an interesting story to tell."

Jones felt something slipping away. He interrupted:

"Earlier police reports suggest they may be deranged."

Sir David shook his head.

"Far from it. You see . . . these children's father, Jack Gunn, is a weather scientist. He was meant to be taking over as Chief Scientist at an experimental station in Upper Hulme – the one that's supposed to be closed. They say their father's been kidnapped and the weather is being manipulated by a group of men including David Harvey, the missing scientist."

"Good God!"

"Furthermore, they know all about Braxton, and have located him for us at the home of a General Sanders, near Luton."

By now, everyone was talking at once. Backs were being slapped. The Prime Minister was beaming. Frank Jones tried his hardest to smile.

"So, what action's being taken?"

The Prime Minister took over.

"Rachel and Matthew Gunn finished telling me their story over two hours ago. I've just received word from the army that the Weather Station has been recaptured. We've got Harvey, a Chief Constable Peters, and three other men. Braxton and Sanders have been in custody for an hour."

"Have you interrogated them?"

"They won't tell us anything. It's unlikely that we'll ever know the full nature of the plot, or all the people involved in it."

"What about the fog?" John Heartstone asked. "Can we get rid of it?"

"Harvey's not being too cooperative. Luckily, we have an expert there already – Mr Gunn, the children's father. He and a Mr Deakin, who was also kept there, are working on it as we speak. They're both groggy after being sedated for six days, but Gunn's going to try and reverse the process Harvey set in motion."

Frank Jones had collected himself.

"Prime Minister, I'm absolutely astounded by the progress you've made this afternoon, how we've escaped from this . . . close call. On behalf of the Cabinet, I would like to offer you and Sir David our most whole-hearted congratulations."

There was a chorus of approval. Jones went on:

"With your permission, I'd like to visit the Research Station personally and talk to Gunn. Make sure it can never happen again."

The Prime Minister was still beaming.

"That sounds an excellent idea, Frank. However, there's one thing I'd like you all to see before you go."

Sir David walked over to a television and video that had been standing, unnoticed, in one corner of the room. The Prime Minister reached into his briefcase and pulled out a videocassette in a BBC case. It was labelled "Prime Ministerial Broadcast".

151

"I have to admit that Sir Anthony wasn't the only person we had followed."

He inserted the tape into the machine. John Heartstone turned and whispered to Frank Jones:

"What on earth do you suppose he's got up his sleeve now?"

Jones shrugged.

"I'm sorry, old man. I haven't the foggiest."

Chapter Seventeen

Rachel held her father's hand as they walked up the hill to the churchyard.

"Could it ever happen again?"

"Not now we know how they did it. Every government in the world read the story in the papers. They wouldn't allow themselves to be blackmailed as ours was."

They reached the churchyard. From here, on a clear day, you could see their cottage in Nether Hulme, and even the tip of the satellite dish which poked above the trees that surrounded the Weather Station, in Upper Hulme.

"You know, Dad, I'm getting scared now, about the pollution and everything. I thought that we'd caused the fog. A lot of people thought that. And now that it's all right again – well, they'll just stop thinking about it, won't they?"

Jack Gunn leant down and looked at her thoughtfully. "You're right to be worried. People are fickle. They get bored with issues after a while. But you know what your mother would have said, don't you? 'They'll only forget if you let them forget.' "

Rachel smiled. It was good that Dad could talk about Mum again. A light drizzle fell on the church-yard, spitting on the faces of the mourners. Rachel looked over at the tired old man who was Prime Minister. Next to him stood a woman from another party, the one who everyone said would replace him after next week's General Election. Matt pointed at her.

"What about the new government, Dad? Will that make a difference?"

Dad shrugged.

"It might. But only if people keep putting the pressure on them all the time. You can't leave things to politicians. You have to start with your own life – change the way you live. Then talk to the people around you, like your mum tried to do. I used to find it threatening, the way she'd lecture me on the things I was supposed to know about. But she was right. You've got to believe that *you* can make a difference."

Yes, thought Rachel. Believe it even if it turned out not to be true, the way people put their faith in religion or politics. You had to try to save the planet, no matter how soppy or trendy or stupidly idealistic that sounded.

Rachel looked at the landscape. Despite the clouds and rain, the countryside around her was beautiful. Stone must have loved it. He'd chosen to stay, after all. If he hadn't, none of them would be here now. And she'd never even said thank you.

The clergyman began the eulogy. Dad had spoken for Stone, when no family could be found. He'd insisted that Stone wouldn't have wanted a military funeral, that a private cremation was more appropriate. There was no way he could keep God out of it, though. Rachel wasn't sure that Stone believed in God: wasn't sure that she did, either. The clergyman was saying:

"A brave and good man, no matter what we think of the way he chose to live. A man who fought for his country and came to her aid at a time of dire need. He showed us that hope can come from the most unlikely places."

Would Stone have done it all again, Rachel wondered, if he knew the cost? Probably. She looked over at the politicians, whose careers they'd saved. If it hadn't been for Dad, would Rachel have risked her life? She didn't know.

"So now, as we gather to scatter his ashes over the fields that he loved . . ."

Her father was holding out the urn. Rachel tried to focus on the object through the tears that were streaming down her face. She put her hand inside.

"Thank you."

There was a light breeze in the air. Rachel threw a handful of ashes into it and passed the urn to her brother.

Later, they walked away from the funeral, father, daughter and son, arm in arm. From the top of the hill, you could see the cars moving along the motorway, all six lanes full. Just beyond them were the seven giant chimneys of the power station, each one smoking. The weather, Rachel noticed, was unusually mild for January.